Dove on the Waters

BY THE SAME AUTHOR

FICTION
The New Zealanders
Summer Fires and Winter Country
Among the Cinders
The Presence of Music
This Summer's Dolphin
An Ear of the Dragon
Strangers and Journeys
A Touch of Clay
Danger Zone
The Lovelock Version
Season of the Jew
Monday's Warriors
The House of Strife

AUTOBIOGRAPHY
One of Ben's

DRAMA
Once on Chunuk Bair

NON FICTION
New Zealand: Gift of the Sea (with Brian Brake)
The Shell Guide to New Zealand
Love and Legend
The Reader's Digest Guide to New Zealand (with Brian Brake)
Voices of Gallipoli

Dove on the Waters

Maurice Shadbolt

BLOOMSBURY

First published in Great Britain 1997

This paperback edition published 1998

Bloomsbury Publishing Plc, 38 Soho Square, London W1V 5DF

A CIP catalogue record for this book
is available from the British Library

ISBN 0 7475 3501 9

Printed in Great Britain by Clays Limited, St Ives plc

There are two tales in the tale: the tale told by the tale and the telling of what the tale tells. It adds up in fact to much more than two tales.

— Jacques Roubard

With gratitude again to Elspeth, and to the memory of Renee Shadbolt, Ada Shadbolt and Luke Perham

PART ONE

Dove on the Waters

GREAT-AUNT ALICE'S memories of Walter Dove were crumbling by the time I panned them for gold. It had been Alice's hope to chronicle Walter herself. Finally she confessed herself unlikely to make anything of her recollections. This was another way of saying that her ninetieth birthday was now behind her. Nevertheless she had no intention of allowing me to meddle negligently with such of her past as involved Walter. She dismissed my complaint that I had too few facts to fill gaps in his story. If I pressed too hard, for too much, she grew terse. 'You,' she reminded me, 'are supposed to be the writer. A few missing facts should exercise your fancy. Where's this famous imagination of yours?'

Well, where was it? And where is it now?

At the beginning of the 20th century Walter Dove was a respected New Zealand lawyer, a mild-mannered and mostly unobtrusive citizen of colonial Auckland. Fastidious to the point of leaving his clients frantic, he never missed a slipshod clause in a contract. Scandal never attached to him, nor alarming aberrance. His wholesome reputation was enhanced by the fact that he scrupulously avoided work involving marital hostilities. Moreover, he never took a criminal case unless he saw a fleck of grace in the alleged malefactor. (Sporadic church attendance would do.) When representing wronged women, he left robust jurymen moist-eyed. These shows of virtue discomforted associates; on the other hand he left cynical laymen persuaded that lawyers were not necessarily rogues. According to Alice his later notoriety came from a cloudless sky.

In 1900 Auckland was home to five hundred gas lamps and fifty thousand people. A city in name if not yet in earnest, it was barely past its frontier beginnings. A canyon of robust stone buildings now hinted at permanence. Astride a lumpy isthmus, lapped by the tides of two large harbours, this unpretentious outpost of Britain remained wedded more to nature than man. ('Last, loneliest, loveliest, exquisite, apart,' romanced Rudyard Kipling on his one reconnaissance.)

The city's legal fraternity was negligible in number, parochial in outlook and clubby in character. Uncomfortable with shop talk and unpractised in gossip, Walter rubbed shoulders with few in his profession and fewer outside it. On occasion, when vocational rites demanded, Walter allowed himself to be seen in the company of colleagues at the vine-wreathed Northern Club, a stocky three-storey building in an enclave of colonial architecture just a short walk from the courts. (Globe-trotting Anthony Trollope had stayed there and praised its surprisingly civilised amenities.) Such social occasions confirmed that Walter was an indifferent mixer; he was often seen heading for the door after one drink and two or three handshakes. On the other hand he was the kind of endearingly eccentric Victorian gentleman relatives delight in recalling. For much of the 20th century no New Zealand living room was complete without a forefather like Walter heroically attempting a smile from a silver frame on an antique sideboard. In life Walter Dove was a man who smiled sparingly and laughed reluctantly. An unhappy man? Alice never offered her thoughts on the subject; she found the question both irritating and irrelevant.

Alice met Walter when the first of her four husbands died young, leaving her with tiny twin daughters, Lucy and Jane. Her husband's confused affairs were in Walter's hands. There were unwise investments and callous creditors. Walter's distress was apparent. There were tut-tuttings and hisses of breath as he laboured through documents. 'There might,' he reported, 'be enough left to pay for the funeral.'

There wasn't. Though Alice didn't learn so till later, Walter picked up the undertaker's bill. He also arranged the sale of Alice's house and settled her in a dwelling suiting her reduced circumstances.

One way and another her husband's estate was cleared of claims. Finally Walter gave her employment too.

Women were still an uncommon sight in legal offices. Responsible solely to Walter, Alice proved a competent clerk. She was also, by the measure of any era, an eye-catching one: surviving photographs show a shapely, stylish and warm-eyed girl. (Her undisguised regard for Walter made for rumour, but it foundered on the fact of his rectitude.) Familiar with Walter's concerns, she could be relied on to discourage visitors when his left hand was conferring with his right. In intermittent form, these solo tête-à-têtes possibly predated Alice's appearance in the office. They became an institution, however, after her advent. At two on Friday afternoons Walter's door closed and his working week ended. He emerged from retreat three hours later, clapped his bowler hat on his head, picked up umbrella and briefcase, wished Alice a happy weekend with Lucy and Jane, and caught the 5.30 ferry across Auckland's Waitemata harbour to the marine suburb of Devonport.

There public knowledge of the man stopped. Walter's domestic life was a mystery. Some recalled his wife visiting the office on her way to a funeral. They remembered a tall and haughty woman with hair heaped high under a veiled hat. She spent fewer than five minutes in her husband's office before speeding him away. This vignette suggested that she found Walter's legal exertions of little interest. It was also possible to deduce that she found her husband poor company. Aside from this somewhat phantasmal visitation, little was known of the woman. It was understood that there were no children of the marriage. Something might be made of that. But as Walter pointed out to juries, suspicion is not evidence.

There were portents. Alice later confessed that she preferred not to examine them. One Friday, for example, Walter failed to close his office door at the customary hour. Perhaps the catch was defective; perhaps it was uncharacteristic carelessness. Alice didn't have her eye on the office clock that afternoon. Seeing his door ajar, and imagining there must be minutes to spare before two, she burst into his office with an urgent document. What met her gaze was breathtaking. His office floor was carpeted with maps. All the world's continents were there in their oceanic setting. Walter was on his hands and knees among the maps. Shoes and socks had been discarded, and his trousers were rolled up his lean shanks. Jacket and tie were absent too. And there was a handkerchief knotted around his neck in seafarer's fashion. Altogether absorbed, he was pencilling a note in the vicinity of the Cape of Good Hope. Then he became aware of intrusion.

'Alice,' he said.

'Mr Dove,' she said.

They looked at each other in astonishment.

'I imagine you have something to say,' he decided.

Poor Alice was dumb; she was still trying to reconcile workaday Walter with this unseemly apparition on all fours. The urgency of Alice's document was lost on her employer. He rose from the floor and arranged himself more respectably. Finally and briskly he rolled up the maps. Alice remained mute.

'You were not meant to see this,' he said.

'I imagine not,' Alice said.

'Nor is it incumbent on you to say you have,' he added.

'You have my word,' she volunteered.

'Lest you wonder, I have always placed great store in the cartographer's trade.'

Alice was not sure she heard right. 'The cartographer's trade?' she said weakly.

'Few of us are without some form of vice,' Walter informed her enigmatically. 'For some it is alcohol or tobacco. For others, gambling on horses or cards. Mine is the magic of maps. Maps, Alice. In maps are dreams. A hundred lands and a thousand dreams.'

Alice accepted this. She had to. A minute later she was at her desk and Walter behind a secure door. It was never again ajar at two on Friday.

That was in 1901. Though Alice did her best not to notice, further symptoms of flux became apparent. When entering his office, even if she knocked, Alice frequently discovered Walter in daydream, his back to the door, gazing through a window with a wide marine view. His hands together as if in prayer, he appeared to be meditating on Auckland's busy harbour and the breezy Pacific beyond. On such occasions she had the impression that he couldn't look her in the face. She learned to live with this. In Alice's charitable view a little idiosyncrasy improved lacklustre males as they aged. A few homely peculiarities made them vastly more interesting. In his middle forties, Walter was hardly old. His unruly mane of white hair, however, made him look more than fifty.

His work was not noticeably affected by his lengthy musings; he remained as punctilious as ever in matters concerning his clients. Alice wondered whether she should say something to one of Walter's partners, lest his condition was signalling mental disorder. In the end she thought not. If his work could not be faulted, why tell? It could be construed as disloyalty. Alice was never less than loyal. And his partners were unlikely to deduce more than she did.

Shaking off such a spell, he once asked abruptly: 'What do you think, Alice?' He was evidently conscripting her for some interior conflict; anyway she was at a loss to reply.

'About what?' she finally said.

'Do you see me as a decent sort of fellow?'

'That is one way of putting it, perhaps.'

'How would you put it?'

'I would see you as worthy. Principled. And honourable.'

This was insufficient for Walter; he wasn't angling for commonplace compliments. 'What I am asking,' he explained patiently, 'is whether I play fair by the world.'

'By the world?'

'Exactly.'

'I should think so,' she said with emphasis.

'Then let me phrase a different question,' he went on. 'Does the world play fair by me?'

Alice found this even more baffling. 'I imagine you are the best judge of that, Mr Dove, ' she said.

'Perhaps it has to be spurred along a little,' he mused. 'What do you think?'

'Spurred along?' she asked.

'Pricked and prodded,' he confirmed. 'What do you think?'

Alice failed to determine what she was thinking and, more to the point, what Walter was.

That conversation preceded Walter's land purchase. Alice learned of it when papers relating to the transaction crossed her desk. The purchase was mystifying. For one thing it was ludicrously small, three or four scrubby acres threaded with tidal shallows and powerfully scented with marine decay. His on payment of five pounds, it was nevertheless no steal. Bordered by mangroves and murky water, the property was some miles up harbour from Auckland. There were no roads and no near neighbours. Access was by bridle path or flat-bottomed dinghy. Beefy pioneers with axe and saw had earlier pitched camp there, levelling the forest which once grew primevally sombre about the upper harbour. There were the remains of a mill which once turned venerable New Zealand kauri into honey-coloured timber. Silence was now the most conspicuous feature of the location. Crabs were audible, people never. There wasn't a dejected client in sight, and distinctly no woman.

Then there was the boat. Alice likewise learned of this when papers concerning its acquisition fell on her desk. A forty-foot, gaff-rigged cutter with sleek line, it had been built as a harbour racer in the 1880s. It bore the unpromising name *Albatross*. Doubly skinned with kauri, fastened with copper rivets, it was at least in seaworthy shape. But what did Walter want with a sailboat? If nothing else this venture helped explain his land transaction. 'To catch a bird,' says a proverb, 'first find a cage.' His half-submerged land was the cage; *Albatross* the bird. The boat was delivered up harbour, moored in his private archipelago, and eventually lifted into wooden cradle for a refit. Tradesmen camped nearby were soon sheathing its hull with copper. This was the customary protection against worm damage in tropical waters. But *Albatross* wasn't resident in tropical waters or in danger of worm damage. What was he up to?

The mystery didn't last. An indifferent prevaricator, Walter finally admitted his intention to the intrigued tradesmen in his employ. One presumably passed the news on. Whatever its source, the story sent a ripple through Auckland's boating community. The fact that Walter had no standing in that salty brotherhood made the matter even more curious. The ripple reached further. The *New Zealand Herald*, one sunny Monday, led off local news with the headline: *Aucklander Plans Solo Circumnavigation of the Globe: City Lawyer Refuses to Speak*. Walter's secret was out. He was quoted as saying that the proposed voyage was a personal matter; that there was no more to be said. But of course there was. Otherwise I should not be struggling to get this down on paper more than ninety years later. Unsurprisingly perhaps, Walter was late for work that day. The delay may have been due to his being as engrossed in the report as any *Herald* reader. He might also have been notifying Mrs Dove of a pleasing reprieve from matrimony.

Everyone in the office was privy to the news by the time Walter arrived; there was a simmering circle of people about an already crumpled copy of the *Herald*. The group dispersed. Desks were reoccupied swiftly, with discreet shuffling and coughing. With mumbled greetings to subordinates, Walter went to his room. There was an awed pause. Finally a bell tinkled. This bell sat on his desk. It meant Alice was needed in his office. Aware of resentful whispers to her rear, Alice presented herself to her employer. 'Close the door,' he ordered. This Alice apprehensively did.

He was quick to the point. 'I daresay, Alice, that you, like most of Auckland, are aware of the tidings in this morning's newspaper.'

'It is impossible not to be, Mr Dove,' Alice said.

'I imagine you may also have an opinion on that report.'

'Not until I hear such news from you,' she explained. 'The report might not be accurate. It might be based on a misunderstanding.'

'It is tolerably truthful,' he informed her.

'In that case,' Alice said, 'I prefer to believe that you know what you are doing.'

'I trust so too,' he said.

He did not make conversation easy. Finally he said, 'Feel at liberty to refer to the subject in my presence. Let me put one fear to rest. Your employment will continue. You will share responsibility for my personal affairs, especially those involving Mrs Dove. These duties will not be demanding. On my return all will be as before.'

'That is most generous,' Alice said. After a difficult pause she added, 'There is one matter which troubles me.'

'And what might that be?'

'What, Mr Dove, if you fail to return?'

'But I shall,' Walter said.

Alice heard unwarranted confidence. She protested, 'It is a dangerous world.'

'Danger is all in the mind,' he told her. 'One cannot see it. One cannot taste or touch it.'

'But the world is real enough,' she argued.

'That also remains to be seen,' he replied.

In the course of the morning his two partners marched into his office. Raised voices were heard. 'Since when did you know the difference between port and starboard?' one challenged. The atmosphere in the office had an electric crackle; the sound of pens on paper could not have been fainter.

Within a week, though, the firm of McDowell, McDonald and Dove began to live with its implausible delinquent. Without hoisting a sail Walter Dove had become a celebrity. Journalists remained intrusive. He was pointed out as he walked in the street. Fellow passengers on the Devonport ferry nudged each other when he boarded. As he tidied his affairs and put the minds of valued clients to rest, his absences from the office became frequent and long. Much of this truancy had to do with lessons in seamanship; he was paying an old salt to supervise him as he excursioned up and down the Waitemata harbour. This proved extremely profitable for the crusty veteran. Another ancient mariner patiently put Walter through a course on the sextant, throwing in every wisp of navigational knowledge he could muster. This conscientious fellow judged rightly that Walter needed all the seafaring wisdom he could win. An inquisitive spectator fleet began following Walter as he took his tutorials. There was laughter sometimes, and unkind jeers. Many wagered on Walter succumbing to the inoffensive Waitemata before he made the acquaintance of the cold-hearted Pacific.

Alice remained fearful, more so when Walter, after months of meditation, announced a departure date: September 21, 1902. He couldn't disavow the project now without losing face. Nor did he mean to disappoint entranced fellow citizens. Walter nosed *Albatross* down harbour with modest competence and moored her on the Auckland waterfront, at the foot of Queen Street, then as now the city's main thoroughfare. There it rocked lightly while Walter stowed provisions and hard-wearing sails aboard.

His audience was now to be numbered in the thousands. Walter's critics became even more vehement. They pointed out that *Albatross* had been built for speed in sheltered water; that it was never designed to duel with ocean. Its sheer was such that there was little more than a foot of freeboard amidships. So frisky a vessel would never survive the Roaring Forties, the perils of which continued to leave Walter unmoved. The enterprise, they asserted, was more than just foolhardy; it was a fancy form of suicide.

Optimists, however, prevailed over pessimists. Most Aucklanders saw a tale likely to bewitch their grandchildren. To enrich their fireside sagas and cheer their favourite away they thronged the waterfront on September 21.

It was a bright spring afternoon. Whatever their reservations about the venture, the city's leading citizens refused to let the occasion pass without prolonged oratory. The mayor stressed that the 20th century was in its infancy and still sadly short of heroes. The mayor also recalled great British voyagers of the past, from Francis Drake to Captain Cook. Walter Dove, he argued, was of the same courageous stuff. Nor was the father of solo voyaging forgotten: Joshua Slocum's classic, *Sailing Alone Around the World*, had only just been published. His companionless triumph was fresh in memory. 'Let it be known,' the mayor said, 'that our little land has its own Joshua Slocum, a man second to none in determination.' Had Walter Dove been inspired by Slocum, as many suspected? If so he wasn't saying. Whatever his inspiration Walter was to be no South Sea facsimile of the sea-hermit Yankee; he was to provide an even more engrossing spectacle. (Not until later was a cynic heard observing that the New Englander and the New Zealander had unsympathetic wives in common: their shrewish womenfolk, it was said, must have made the sea's discomforts seem slight.)

There were few daylight hours left for *Albatross* to clear the harbour for its baptismal brush with the Pacific. There were final handshakes. Legal colleagues were among those gruffly extending good wishes. The notable absentee was Mrs Dove. Alice substituted for Walter's missing spouse with a kiss and a bouquet of roses. 'Come back,' she whispered in his ear.

'I mean to,' he said with impressive conviction.

On the mayor's call, there were three booming cheers for the daring Aucklander. Mooring lines were cast off and recovered by Walter. Sail was hoisted as *Albatross* drifted out from the wharf into uncluttered water. Observers noted that his footwork aboard was not altogether nimble. Reticent to the last about his course, Walter was away.

A flotilla of cordial yachtsmen trailed him for a time. Alice was aboard one of the craft which kept Walter company as far as North Head, the onetime Maori hilltop fortress which overlooks the entrance to Waitemata harbour. There were spectators along the shore, women waving scarves and handkerchiefs. One by one, as they met chilly breeze and choppy water, his waterborne well-wishers melted away. Shoreline spectators thinned too, until only one was visible. It was a middle-aged woman, walking the Devonport seafront as if attempting to keep pace with Walter's vessel. It had to be Mrs Dove, and was. There was no fond call across the water, no arm lifted in farewell. She was seen walking slowly homeward.

Daylight was ebbing as Walter pointed *Albatross* away from Auckland and into the Pacific. Her sails filled auspiciously; waves cracked over her hull as she found wind. The first mile was behind; the most optimistic assessment said there were 23,999 more before he saw New Zealand again. Walter was at last alone with the earth's heaving waters. Alice said she found her heart filling her throat. 'He looked so little and the world so large,' she remembered. Sixty years later a tear slowly formed and suddenly fell.

No one expected to hear from Walter in a hurry. Increasingly many did not expect to hear from him at all. Months without a word were therefore no surprise. These were the days, it needs to be stressed, when there was no radio, no marine bands, no earth-circling satellites ferrying information to seafarers. Those abroad on the ocean had to win intelligence from cloud and horizon, wind and wave. Should they misread the messages therein, there could be no SOS, Mayday call, or last words to loved ones. They would descend mute to their death.

Any communique from Walter in the short term was unlikely. He had last been seen heading east, perhaps toward South America. There is no land of significance between New Zealand and the Americas. Walter's rudimentary knowledge of navigation ensured that he had small chance of locating the little which did. There was virtually nowhere to off-load letters to Auckland. Perhaps, shunning caution, he had simply hurled himself south into the Roaring Forties; perhaps he was still contemplating the dramatic silhouettes of Tierra del Fuego, or battling with towering waves and treacherous icebergs in the vicinity of Cape Horn. For optimists there was always the possibility that some vessel calling into Auckland might set ashore a bruised, heartbroken and skeletal Walter, lately and luckily retrieved from the Pacific's jaws. Such a return would not be altogether ignoble. At least his survival would confound his critics; at least he would be alive.

Nervous Alice made her first call on Mrs Dove the day after Walter's departure. She took a ferry across the harbour and found a modest Victorian cottage on the seafront. Sinister ceramic gnomes leered from pansies in the front garden. Climbing roses wreathed the door. She anticipated a weeping wreck of a woman within. This was not the case. Mrs Dove was composed, dry-eyed, even cheerful. Alice found this difficult to manage. Serenity seemed callous with Walter just a day gone; Alice herself was still shaky. Sensing this, Mrs Dove benevolently poured her visitor a sherry.

'Well?' she said. 'Do you think he'll be back?'

'We must pray so,' Alice said.

'*You* may pray,' Mrs Dove said. 'I fear I cannot.'

Alice, a good Anglican, was shocked. 'Cannot?'

'Should I need to fall to my knees, the Lord will hear no plea for Walter's well-being.'

Alice began seeing a monster.

'My one prayer,' Mrs Dove disclosed, 'would be that he is satisfied.'

'Satisfied? In what sense?'

'In the sense that he has what he needs. Naturally I wish Walter well so long as he remains lost to view. His needs do not include me. They never have.'

'I see,' Alice said.

There was a significant silence. If there was grief in the woman, she had buried it deep.

'You are fond of my husband,' she suggested.

'I am not alone in that,' Alice replied evasively.

'But you, I think, especially,' Mrs Dove said. 'Your face says it all.'

Alice tried and failed to rearrange her current expression. 'I am much in debt to Mr Dove,' she allowed. 'I have never met a man I respect more.'

'Not even your late husband?'

Alice was slow to answer. 'Not even he,' she admitted.

Mrs Dove decided her point made; she changed course a few degrees. 'It has been difficult for everyone,' she said. 'And most of all Walter.'

'I thought him remarkably assured, these past months,' Alice said. 'He refused to hear mockery and laughter.'

'Why should he?' Mrs Dove asked. 'He is now free.'

'Free?' Alice queried. 'My impression is that he has made himself slave to wind and water.'

'I am talking of the strain of seeming worthy. I daresay you have never considered what it might have cost him to win the esteem of others.'

This was true. Alice hadn't. The notion was new. Wordless, she began seeing Walter afresh.

'Nor,' Mrs Dove added unkindly, 'were you to be aware of his weakness for a pretty face.'

Quick to her feet, now unable to leave soon enough, Alice explained that she would visit Mrs Dove regularly and see her comfortably in pocket. Mrs Dove had surprisingly little interest in the monetary details. 'So you will come again?'

'Once weekly,' Alice promised.

'Good,' Mrs Dove said. 'I mean to play bridge with friends on Monday, Wednesday and Friday. Otherwise I shall be available to visitors. Walter, you see, is not the only one free. I imagine the wicked old fake expects me to be grateful.'

'Wicked? Mr Dove?' Alice was not up to larger protest.

'Your innocence is most moving,' Mrs Dove observed.

Such was Alice's version of the encounter. Nothing suggests that she failed Mrs Dove.

More months passed, then all of a year. There was still no whisper from Walter. Not from South America, North America, or anywhere else on the globe. One spurious tale had him dwelling half-naked among the mighty icons of Easter Island. Another as absurd had him revelling with the descendants of Bounty mutineers on minuscule Pitcairn. The first anniversary of his departure — or disappearance — was marked by a newspaper article under the heading: *The Mystery of the Albatross*. This argued that there was still room for hope, but not much. It soon seemed that Alice alone had faith. The virtually unanimous view was that Walter had perished. Boating authorities were quoted at length. Most heartlessly asserted that Walter had courted disaster; that he had himself to blame. Dilettantes, they said, had no place on the great waters of the world; Walter Dove's ill-starred voyage served best as a cautionary tale. Nevertheless there was a crowded memorial service in the Anglican cathedral, followed by a wake organised by onetime legal colleagues in the Northern Club. Walter was recalled with respect and frequently with affection at these functions. He was too long gone for tears. And though a dark-dressed Mrs Dove was present in the cathedral, she made no attempt to play grieving widow. Nor did she exchange words with mourners more saddened. She was last seen scuttling off to her ferry.

The second anniversary of his enterprise arrived with an article headed in lesser font: *No Sign of City Seafarer*. This curtly recorded what most now knew. Optimism could no longer be justified. Not a paragraph appeared on the third anniversary: it had all been said. From time to time, when mystery wreckage was reported — on the New Zealand coast or elsewhere in the Pacific — Walter Dove was newsworthy again for a week. None of the wreckage, however, could be identified as fragments of *Albatross*. Nor did the occasional castaway seaman, uplifted from sub-antarctic island or equatorial atoll, answer to the name Dove. The lawyer was now lore.

Six years later, or the year after Walter was determined dead for legal purposes, and his will put into effect, that was still the case. Auckland's population had doubled to a hundred thousand. The city now possessed a tall town hall and the largest single-span arch bridge in the world. Suburbs were grabbing up free land. Orchards and vineyards were sweetening unkempt outskirts. By 1910 Auckland was barely recognisable as the city Walter Dove had left. Mrs Dove, no longer reliant on her husband's hand-outs, now with considerable capital of her own, lived in a grand house on the Devonport seafront. Her bridge parties had become famous. So had the accumulations of empty gin bottles put out for rubbish collectors. Alice and her daughters were also beneficiaries of Walter's will. This meant a new dwelling and a modest income. She resigned her job, when it became tactful to do so — that is, when Walter was lawfully dead and Mrs Dove no longer in need of a weekly visitor. Never lacking men friends, Alice once or twice contemplated marriage. On balance she felt widowhood desirable until her daughters were adult. With time on her hands, however, she turned back to law. She enrolled at Auckland university and became one of the first New Zealand women to win a law degree. Uncomfortable male colleagues swiftly perceived her as a menace to their profession. They were right. If women were to be allowed the run of a courtroom, no male citadel was safe. Where might it end? With unseemly feminine laughter in the precincts of the Northern Club, perhaps.

On a summer day in 1910 two teenage canoeists, in search of adventure, were paddling their leaky, home-made craft through the upper reaches of the Waitemata. That day they had more drama than they bargained for. Squeezing through mangrove forest, forcing aside stiff foliage, they found themselves in an unfamiliar stretch of water. Magically sequestered there was a vessel of substance. They cruised closer to investigate. Its name, barely legible among peeling paint, meant nothing to the boys. They had more interest in the apple, plum and peach trees set back from the tideline and generously screening the approach to the boat. The boys beached their canoe and crept stealthily into this appetising oasis. At that point a discharged shotgun made their day memorable. No matter that the shot was directed at predatory birds. They paddled off fast.

One of the boys, at family dinner that night, reported their discovery.

'A ship up there?' his father said.

'An old cutter,' the boy confirmed

'A wreck?'

'Almost sunk. And there's a guard with a gun.'

'It could be stolen. You notice its name?'

'*Albatross*,' the boy remembered.

His father was thoughtful. 'That,' he said, 'rings a bell.'

With his son as guide and a friendly constable as companion he rowed up the estuary the next day. When they ran out of tide, they abandoned their dinghy and floundered through knee-deep mud. After more turns in the maze, however, they found themselves viewing a mirage-like vessel all but high and dry among mangroves. There was a second surprise, this time in the form of a deeply tanned man of middle years with a magnificent head of white hair. Shirtless, with ragged trousers rolled to the knee, he was viewing his visitors with a whimsical eye. 'Welcome aboard, gentlemen,' he said. He directed them to a gangway and courteously extended a helping hand to each. 'You aren't unexpected,' he informed them.

'Us?' the constable said.

'Someone was bound to be along,' the fellow insisted. 'If not in one year, then another.'

'It seems to me that explanation is in order,' the suspicious constable said. 'To the best of our memory a vessel named *Albatross* went missing, with its skipper, some years ago.' The constable deduced that the matter was far from trivial. The mangrove-dweller might be a murderous felon who had cached himself away after disposing of his skipper. A pirate, no less.

'Missing?' the fellow said mildly. 'This boat?'

'Indeed,' the constable said.

'Unless appearances deceive,' the fellow went on, 'it's still doing honest service here.'

'You agree, then, that we are talking about one and the same vessel ?'

'I imagine we are,' the stranger said.

'Then perhaps you could favour us with your name.'

'Guess,' Walter Dove said.

'A cheerful old cove,' the constable reported to a superior.

'And where's he been all this time?'

'Afloat, he says.'

With wind of a sensation, the press raced into conjecture. *Forgotten Voyager's Shy Return*, announced one breathless journal. *Miraculous Survival of Modest Aucklander*, declared another. Their editors would soon rue every word.

Alice remembered the world coming to a halt when she read the news. Neighbourhood noise faded. Birds became songless. Walter had done it after all. Walter, as promised, was back. She sat down slowly, newspaper in hand, and (I surmise) wept. She found it impossible to speak to her two lively daughters when they bounced in from school.

For a time Alice knew no more than any other inhabitant of Auckland. She thought it prudent not to contact Walter until uproar ebbed. Meanwhile the tidal reaches of the upper Waitemata filled with cruising sightseers hoping for a glimpse of *Albatross* and the man who sailed her. Many went aground; most returned foiled, soiled and profane. The few who did find her had much to puzzle over. Oysters flecked her hull. Rust and rot were rife and rigging frayed. Further, a few furled shreds of mildewed canvas seemed to be all that was left of the vessel's sail. In short, there was much to suggest that *Albatross* was not newly ensconced in the estuary. This meant one of two things. That Walter had survived with unprecedented help from Providence; or that he had never cleared the New Zealand coast.

Cries of foul began drowning cheers. More so when a rural storekeeper, a mile or two inland, identified Walter as an occasional customer for years. As scepticism mounted Walter preserved a stiff silence. There was no reason for him to contribute his twopence worth to the controversy. No word of a lie had been uttered nor deceit intended; he had been afloat these past seven years, and no one could say different.

There was one further headline before Walter faded from the newspapers: *Yachting Riddle Irks Aucklanders*. It continued to vex many, though never Alice. After some indecision she wrote a note to Walter and hoped some resourceful postman would seek him out. She had a reply after four tense days. 'Please come,' he said with urgency.

Alice had a male friend willing to arrange an overland excursion to Walter's domain. First there was a smoky train. Then there were plodding horses. Finally they came to Walter's orchard. Nay-sayers had pointed to the well-established trees — lemon and grapefruit, as well as pear, apple and peach — as evidence that Walter had been stationary for almost a decade. On high ground there was a garden where peas, beans, spinach and pumpkin flourished. Everything, in fact, a mariner might need to fight off scurvy. Now the most suspect vessel to have sailed New Zealand waters, *Albatross* sat flightless nearby. It was rolling lightly on rising tide; light rippled on its discoloured hull.

Walter rose beaming from the serene vista. As Alice told it, his seven years of shipboard life had agreed with him; he seemed not to have aged a day. He had an armful of apples, which he spilled on first sight of Alice. He gazed at her speechless as the fruit scattered. Was he thinking on how time had treated her? The apples continued to roll, slowly enough to be counted as lost years of their lives.

'Alice,' he said with unhidden pleasure.

'Mr Dove,' she said.

At this stage in her story Alice became suspiciously reticent. 'You don't need to know everything,' she protested.

'I do,' I assured her.

'People are entitled to privacy,' she claimed. 'Even if decrepit or dead.'

She was in the first category; Walter by then in the second. I assumed she was unwilling to confess that their reunion was an occasion for tears, perhaps even for sobs.

'If you won't tell me, I warned, 'I'll make it up. Fancy might be more irritating than fact.'

'Don't threaten me,' she said angrily.

'All I want,' I pleaded, 'is a clue to what was said that day.'

There was a thoughtful silence. 'Very well, then. There was more unsaid than said.'

'I can imagine.' I said sympathetically.

'Can you? I think not.'

'Go on,' I urged.

Finally she said, 'There were business matters of course. He was literally back from the dead. His estate had been divided and dispersed. As you know, I was a beneficiary. I offered him all I had left of his legacy. My house too. He wouldn't hear of it. He said that the Walter Dove who dictated that will was long deceased. Heaven knows what arrangement, if any, he came to with Mrs Dove. She remained the wealthiest woman on the Devonport seafront. Her bridge parties became bigger still, giving her even more of a chance to show off her jewellery. Walter on the other hand scrimped and scraped, selling his fruit and vegetables and somehow managing.'

'So it's a sad story,' I suggested.

'If you're talking money,' Alice said.

She didn't volunteer more. Finally I asked, 'Is there anything else I am permitted to know?'

'Just that curiosity killed the cat,' she said.

'I don't see the point of that proverb in present circumstances,' I claimed.

'No?' she said with indifference.

'No,' I said, feebly standing my ground.

'Then a timely reminder seems in order. Even as an infant you were inquisitive to the point of gross impudence. I see no improvement.'

'Can we get on with it now?' I asked in desperation.

'Very well, then. He asked after Lucy and Jane. He wanted my girls to holiday with him.'

'Why Lucy and Jane?'

'You know perfectly well,' she asserted.

'Remind me,' I appealed.

'After his years of solo voyaging he was weary of his own company. He needed crew. First Lucy and Jane. Then you, when you came along. Of course you remember.'

'Not much,' I claimed. 'Just a half-naked old man shouting and racing around the deck. There was always pandemonium.'

This wasn't fair. Nor was it true. To part Alice from her memories, however, I was obliged to sham having few of my own; I had to be provocative.

'It is my understanding,' she said, 'that commotion is not infrequent on the high sea.'

'Alice,' I said patiently, 'we all know his voyaging was fantasy.'

'That, young man, is your view,' she said. 'It is also a libel. I regret Walter isn't here to put you in your place.'

In danger of losing her goodwill, I called that interview off. We never again divided on the authenticity of Walter's voyaging.

On that September day in 1902, after the civic farewell, Walter pointed *Albatross* out of Waitemata harbour and watched floating sympathisers and waterside cheerleaders diminish astern. Even Mrs Dove had flown. What happened then may have been spontaneous.

Did second thoughts of heartstopping character win the day? Or was the manoeuvre long planned? There is evidence to support both propositions.

The outcome was the same. As light began to dim, he modified his course dramatically, tacking away from open sea and doubling back up harbour toward swampy solitude. There was no one to witness this inspired U-turn. Walter must have been careful not to quarrel with moored freighters and harbour ferries along his route. One presumes he dropped anchor at a distance from prying eyes as dusk cloaked Auckland and street-lamps were lit.

With dawn's first glimmer, the city's citizens still dreaming, he would have let the tide carry him the last miles up harbour until he sweetly eased *Albatross* on to something approximating terra firma. As the tide rose higher (by chance or choice September 21 coincided with one of the year's largest tides) Walter roped himself to *Albatross* and towed her foot by foot, inch by inch, yet further into seclusion. There, in a cloud of foliage, he moored her forever. There he remained for the rest of his life. That is, for more than four decades. End of story? Never, Alice would say. Never.

'You always did miss the point,' she added.

The point she was making, and I was missing, was that Walter was no fraud. An illusionist perhaps, an escape merchant who made Houdini look mediocre. But a fraud? Never.

Walter's marshy Eden was soon a second home for Alice and her daughters. Lucy and Jane were with Walter for school holidays. They bunked in the foredeck; Alice, when aboard, in the stern. With female company, Walter camped under canvas on the deck; he also wore clothes, not always his custom.

No matter that the vessel seldom moved more than inches, that never a sail filled with breeze. Walter delighted in playing Captain Bligh, roaring orders into high wind as ocean foamed around them. There was no mutter of mutiny from his crew. They loyally survived polar tempest and tropic hurricane; they drifted in equatorial calms under starlit sky. Lucy and Jane were soon reading charts, familiarising themselves with perilous shores, and determining their next port of call. When the pirates of the Celebes Sea weren't menacing, and whale herds no hazard off the Falklands, Walter left the girls with the helm while he prepared nourishing meals on the kerosene stove in his galley. His no-frill cuisine was based on vegetables from his garden and fish netted from neighbouring creeks. His originality in the galley was reserved for enterprises with rotten apples. Years before the world heard of penicillin, Walter persuaded himself of the life-enhancing properties of mould. He ate only blackening morsels of apple, discarding anything remotely rosy. He even let his porridge grow fungus before devouring it with relish. Jars of vegetable matter, in advanced states of disrepair, filled galley shelves. From these he devised remedies which people later swore by. Hardy Walter was testimony to his own medication. He simply ceased ageing, especially with Lucy and Jane aboard.

How often did they circumnavigate the globe with Walter in those spellbinding years? Even Joshua Slocum managed it only the once. They lost track after the first score circuits. There was an end to it, of course. Lucy and Jane soon left adolescence behind; they were suddenly young ladies with another life on land. Male friends began to make an appearance. Two turned into husbands. Then came babies. Difficulty of access meant the girls visited less and annually at most. So passed the 1920s. In that decade middle-aged Alice judged herself ready for matrimony again. She finally exchanged vows with a banker of sober and practical disposition, a man seemingly both safe and solvent. The flaw in the arrangement, not detected until after their nuptials, was that he was as opinionated as Alice. In other respects too he fell short of expectation, not least when he expressed his wish that she abandon the courtroom for the kitchen; he couldn't have associates saying that he lived off his wife. The end, never far off from the first day of marriage, finally came when he raised objections to her continuing concern for Walter. He couldn't see what she saw in the failed imposter. Later in life, in response to my impudent query, she failed to recall how her second marriage happened. Her one attempt at explanation was not especially persuasive. 'I rather think I felt sorry for him,' she decided.

'You?' I said. 'Sorry?'

'Men are quite as entitled as women to have someone feel sorry for them. Life isn't easy for them, as I daresay you know. Not the least of their woes is that they are obliged to put up with women. I wouldn't change sex for all the tea in China, not even all the coffee in Brazil.'

'This is revolutionary, coming from you.'

'I see no reason why I should withhold my sympathies from half the human race.'

There were times when Alice left me speechless. This was one of them. My silence lengthened.

'You were asking to explain my remarriage,' she reminded me.

'I was,' I agreed, leaning forward with anticipation.

'As you may or may not be aware,' she informed me, 'wedlock was once rather the fashion.'

Marital estrangement allowed her freedom to visit Walter more often. Seeing him despondently solo again, she rummaged among relatives for children who might serve as a substitute crew. 'I was a one-woman press gang,' she explained. 'I was like those navy recruiters, in Lord Nelson's time, who biffed unwary men on the head in dark alleys and carried them off senseless to serve their country.'

Alice didn't loiter in dark alleys with the intention of rendering junior relatives unconscious. Nevertheless she had an unsympathetic response from the parents she approached. They had no intention of allowing their little ones to holiday with a lunatic in a waterlogged vessel parked in unlovely swamp. Walter was a proven liar and possibly a paedophile. They were unmoved by Alice's assertion that Walter would broaden the horizons of their offspring as no school could. The answer was always no. Walter remained crewless.

That was still the case when I was born. My young brother bawled into the world soon after. My mother had an enfeebling time of it with his birth. Her condition was compounded by a malevolent spot on her lung. That meant a sanatorium.

With sons to feed and clothe, my father required rescue. Alice stepped in. She announced that she would take charge of my year-old brother. As for me, she knew just the place for a weepy four-year-old. She was, of course, killing two birds with one stone. Walter had a first mate and I had a third parent. And we cruised off together. This had disadvantages. My landlubber parents were soon people in a foreign port of call, speaking an unintelligible tongue. My father was preoccupied with my ailing mother and visited me seldom. My mother was the feeble woman Alice fetched me to see once a month. 'My poor little boy,' my parent would say, beginning to sob.

Poor? Me? Her tears were incomprehensible. I was literally having the time of my life. Huck Finn's adventures with Nigger Jim on the Mississippi, or Sancho Panza's with Don Quixote, were as nothing to mine with Walter. It was a relief to escape the inhospitable sanatorium to rendezvous with Uncle Walter, as he allowed himself called when not at the helm. (On watch he had to be addressed Skipper.) He always arranged an arduous itinerary after a sanatorium visit. My mother's tears would be forgotten as we cruised close to Africa's shadowy shore in humid twilight. 'Smell the wild jungle flowers,' he urged. 'Go on. Smell them.'

I did, and the blooms of Borneo and Tahiti too.

Though memory makes it longer, it seems I crewed with Walter less than two years. I was suddenly of an age for school. My mother was out of the sanatorium. It was time to pack my nautical kit-bag and pick up my seaman's papers (testifying to my competence under sail and recommending me to future employers). As my father and Alice whisked me off in a car (a road having at last breached Walter's fastness) my late skipper stood on the foredeck waving farewell. I imagined I might be back when school and parents permitted. Walter knew better. He knew it was over, his voyaging as much as mine. The decades had taken their toll of ship and skipper. Rot had dug still further into *Albatross*; leaks were many and the deck unsound. As for the skipper, a doctor had diagnosed another kind of decay. In early 1938 Walter Dove disappeared a second time. This journey didn't allow for a U-turn. Obituaries were brief and contradictory. One journalist, confused by old clippings, went so far as to say that Walter Dove had been the least celebrated solo voyager of all time. This was not altogether erroneous. Had Alice or I been asked, we might have said much the same. Meanwhile suburban scavengers boarded and plundered *Albatross* for what it was worth. They found no more than timber and metal.

In the late 1960s, not long before her own life ended, I had an enlightening and sometimes exhilarating week with Alice. I was just back from Europe, after several years away. During those years, to no one's surprise, I materialised as a novelist. Through childhood, adolescence and youth I had been seen by friends and relatives as a resourceful liar, a shifty teller of tales tall enough to overshadow my many shortcomings. My first book, just published in London and New York, confirmed that my storytelling tic was likely incurable.

What did I want from Alice? The makings of a novel? One which drew on a luminous episode of childhood? Though I was never to write it, I must have had one in mind. I had still to admit to Alice that my journeys with Walter continued to colour my life. Perhaps she knew so already. Perhaps she knew, long before I did, that one yarn-spinner had handed the helm to another.

Meanwhile I sat patiently with Alice until she thought to surrender a fact or an old woman's fancy. She delighted in delaying matters. She especially enjoyed outwitting my tape recorder with long pauses and inaudible mutters. Though she wished Walter on record, her feelings were mixed. She had to be persuaded that I would do Walter justice. It worried her that I pried more than seemly. She was, after all, still an Edwardian woman.

'There's something missing,' I complained.

'Like what?'

'Motive,' I said. 'I have no motive for Walter. Nothing to suggest why he did what he did, lived as he lived.'

'No?' she said rather coolly.

'No,' I insisted. 'There has to be more.'

'Authors are a pestilential species,' she announced. 'Why fret about motive? Why prey on the man? He wasn't a murderer.'

'Motive might light my way a little,' I suggested.

She wasn't impressed. 'Was he or was he not a success in what he did?'

'One could argue so,' I said cautiously.

'Then argue so,' she urged. 'When you have lived as long as I have, young man, you realise that human beings, both wise and foolish, seldom make sense. The miracle is that now and then someone does.'

'Meaning Walter did?'

'He did,' she said.

This had finality.

'But there *is* more to it, isn't there?' I persisted.

There was a lengthy silence.

Finally she said, 'Why don't you drive me out there? To Walter's old hideout?'

Though suspecting that this might be a ploy to put me off the scent, I did. Finding the right estuary wasn't easy. The city's population was now a half million and promising to double yet again. A tall bridge now spanned Waitemata harbour. Waterside land had been bulldozed for new suburbs. There were loops of road and patches of low-cost housing. Blundering from one cul-de-sac to another that warm afternoon, we finally sighted familiar contours.

'Here,' she said with authority. 'Stop.'

I parked the car and helped her out. We didn't walk far. Alice wasn't agile enough to descend to sea level. We looked down on the serene backwater where *Albatross* once sat, where Walter Dove whipped up hurricanes, strange lands and high adventure. Alice's one concession to age was a walking stick. She used it with spirit that afternoon, pointing out half-lost landmarks. A few arthritic fruit trees persisted where Walter's orchard and garden formerly prospered. Alice also drew my gaze to scraps of timber, all that was left of *Albatross*, and for that matter of Walter, among aromatic mire. We sat in the shade of a roadside tree and drank tea from a thermos. The day was peaceful. The sound of traffic was indistinct in the distance. There were silent yachts down harbour.

'He's still about,' she decided.

'In a way,' I said tactfully.

There was a long silence.

'What do you have to starboard?' she asked.

'Africa,' I told her. 'Wild jungle flowers. Smell them. Go on.'

She sniffed thoughtfully. 'Indeed,' she decided.

'What do you have to port, then?' I asked.

She was reluctant to say. 'I am not,' she replied, 'going to make this easy for you.'

'I never imagined you were,' I said.

'Good,' she said. 'Ask what you want while I'm tolerable company.'

I plunged in. 'All right,' I said. 'I'll tell you what I think. You tell me where I'm wrong.'

'Very well,' she sighed.

'You were Walter's motive.'

'Me?'

'You.'

To my surprise, she received this in silence.

I went on nervously, 'Walter, from the time he took you under his wing, and into his office, found his longing for you more and more excruciating. And all but impossible to hide.'

'Longing?'

'Lust, then.'

Alice protested, rather weakly, 'Must you? Must you see sex in everything?'

I found the courage to continue. 'I might,' I admitted, 'have said affection. But I think we are talking lust. It would have been Walter's word for his difficulty. It went against the grain of his life. A wife without respect for him made matters even more dire. His marital situation was hopeless; his feeling for you impossible to acknowledge. Aside from anything else, you were in your early twenties, he in his forties. He couldn't have taken advantage of you had he lived a hundred years. I also suspect that, having found the philanderer in himself, he may even have been suicidal. But rather than cut his throat he bought a boat and charted a course to nowhere. It was an enterprising response. Some might say honourable.'

I looked to Alice for confirmation or correction. I found neither.

A lone tear drifted down her face.

'I suppose you think yourself smart,' she said.

We sat on the roadside as the afternoon cooled, as silvery tide found a path through amphibious trees. Alice didn't speak. At length I did.

'There is,' I began, 'something else I shouldn't ask.'

'I can't imagine what it could be,' she said tersely.

'I rather think you do,' I suggested.

'Go on, then. Ask.'

'Was there ever anything between you and Walter?'

'Anything?' she asked.

'Of an intimate nature.'

There I stumbled. There I stopped. Alice, with startling generosity, came to my rescue.

'Make love?' she said. 'Is that what you're asking? Did we ever make love? Is that it?'

'I suppose it is,' I replied weakly.

'The world belongs to the imaginative. That, you may recall, appeared to be Walter's belief.'

'That isn't an answer.'

'Let me put it another way, then. You said there was more to the story. More than you could see.'

'True,' I agreed.

'There was more,' she confessed.

An old woman's hand felt shakily for my chin. She tilted my face upward until my eyes met hers. She was smiling.

'What do you mean by more?' I asked.

'A splendidly libidinous week in the Caribbean,' she said.

PART TWO

The Venetian Bride

SAVE FOR MY great-aunt's need to put me in my place, I would never have learned of Rose Lightfoot.

'Love?' Alice lamented. 'You wouldn't know what it was if you fell over it.'

'Me?' I said.

'Your generation,' she said.

'I refuse to take responsibility for my generation,' I announced.

'I daresay you do,' she said loftily.

Until this jeremiad we had been sitting amiably in her garden in warm Auckland dusk. It was a summer day in the 1960s. The war in Vietnam was fathering uproar in formerly sedate New Zealand streets. Though Alice prided herself on remaining abreast of the times, she continued to confuse that Asian mêlée with the Boer war and coolly dismissed my protests that more than half a century separated the two conflicts. On the other hand she now acknowledged that the British Empire was no longer in business, and that a quartet of Liverpool noise-makers called the Beatles were. (She was on nodding terms with television; nodding, in fact, comprised the greater part of her viewing. Asked why she bothered, she claimed that she was merely confirming that it wasn't worth hanging on for her hundredth birthday.)

That evening's outburst was largely due to my recent divorce, on which she had unshakeable opinions. It was her belief that it was my fault the marriage had foundered. Never mind that there were extenuating circumstances; she declined to acknowledge that my spouse might also have been imperfect. Her reason was selfish. She had rather liked my second wife and was regretting her disappearance. So, in my melancholic way, was I. Alice, true to form, gave cold comfort. She persisted in raining the wisdom of her ninety-plus years on my head.

'If you loved the woman,' she said, 'you wouldn't have let her leave. Bona fide lovers don't abide parting. Not until their last breath, perhaps not even then.'

'Possibly,' I said with caution. I sensed hazard near.

'Definitely,' she said. 'And it is not my intention to brook argument on the subject.'

'I didn't imagine you would,' I said.

'In my day we knew what marriage was for,' she explained. 'Certainly some of us did.'

'Children?' I ventured.

'Desirably,' she said. 'Not necessarily.'

'So what are you talking about?'

'Loyalty,' she explained. 'Devotion. Light in the dark, warmth in the cold. We know that the light will leave; that the cold will win. Marriage allows us a little illusion. It may even ease us through.'

'Through? Through what?'

'Death,' she said.

'Come on,' I said with scepticism. 'Death?'

'If need be, 'she said severely.

I was silent.

'Where do you take comfort now?' she asked.

'Where I always have,' I argued.

'You can't hide in your wretched books forever.'

'Try me and see,' I said perilously.

With monumental irrelevance, she added, 'I imagine you smoke that fancy tobacco in your pipe too.'

I refrained from pointing out that marijuana, if that was what she had in mind, was not akin to tobacco; and not customarily smoked in a pipe. I wasn't *that* wedded to the 1960s. I may even have been the first person in the Western world to feel nostalgic for the prim 1950s.

By now it should be clear that Alice, when in feud with the world, held me to account for most of its failings. Not that I didn't have enough defects to keep her engrossed. I plainly did.

It is time to come clean. Looking back, I realise, more than thirty years late, that Alice was the love of my life. No female of my generation, spouses included, ever measured up to her. She was the woman I might have married. Might? Should. Perhaps Alice felt this too: regret might explain her late-life homilies and thundering non sequiturs. She had long needed me to come to her with my childish tears, my adolescent woes and my adult griefs; she would have felt deprived had I failed her in this respect. She would have been as bereft had I not provided her with stories and novels she could shred without mercy. As a critic she was a gifted sharpshooter; she made most literary assassins seem lightweight wimps. The truth is, however, that I had no more steadfast a fan. When I was out of earshot, or when she imagined I was, she wouldn't hear a word said against me. (She took wayward pride in identifying certain of my characters as modelled on her. She was seldom right and sometimes hair-raisingly wrong.) In theory we made an exemplary couple. There was, however, a problem. It was more than shared ancestry and borderline incest. We were five decades apart in age. I was merely in my thirties; she in her nineties. That made our liaison even more unlikely. She made up for this by befriending my wives and lovers, vicariously living their lives and sharing my bed at second hand. There may have been something unhealthy in this. I fail to see it.

The Auckland evening began to cool, Alice to subside. 'Talking of love,' she said, 'I believe I have never mentioned Rose Lightfoot.'

She was right. I had never heard the name.

'That is a regrettable omission,' she decided.

'In what way?'

'Knowledge of Rose might modify your presently morose view of womankind. Fanciful though it may seem, it might even improve your character.'

'Is this another cautionary tale?'

'Perhaps a touch wholesome for contemporary taste.'

'Meaning what?'

'Don't rush me. It helps, in these matters, if you defer to my age and experience.'

I sighed. 'Go on,' I said.

'If you don't want to hear it, you have only to tell me so bluntly. Just don't mutter "Go on" in that surly tone.'

'I'm not surly,' I protested.

'Let me assure you that my hearing has lately been checked.'

'Not thoroughly enough,' I informed her.

Alice and I could bicker as competently as any married couple.

'There must,' she decided, 'have been a reason for my not mentioning Rose before. Perhaps I sensed that her story would be wasted on you.'

'Alice,' I warned, 'you are becoming impossible again.'

'Good,' she said with relish.

At such times I didn't find it difficult to imagine the fierce young woman who in 1915 or thereabouts had been arrested while speaking at a riotous anti-war meeting, been charged with sedition, and all but disbarred from the legal profession thereafter. The largest loss was her current marriage. Her horrified husband, unable to stand the strain, or cope with the prospect of a convict wife, forsook home, hearth and Alice. It was said that her relative youth and celebrated beauty saved her from incarceration. This was possible. Alice was at her best in a fight, even if it was about not fighting.

In anticipation of the undertaker's overdue knock on her door, she had begun relinquishing her past and burdening me with long-hoarded anecdotes. It wasn't just that she needed someone to tune up her narratives. She was also interested in seeing how fast they turned up in my fiction. Sometimes it took less than a week. Otherwise I was mostly a male shoulder to lean on when she adventured down memory lane. She didn't need to compose memoirs so long as she had a usefully literate acolyte. Her eye for period detail meant that such excursions were seldom less than worthwhile. My knowledge of the Edwardian era, for example, had become encyclopaedic. I also had a fair sense of what life was like for a professional woman

— in Alice's case, for a female lawyer — in the first third of the 20th century. But not until that evening did I have knowledge of the Lightfoot family. Had Alice been respecting a client's confidences? I think not. I suspect she was waiting her chance to land one of her virtuoso blows below the belt. Now that she had next to no male contemporaries to incapacitate, she made do with me.

Lightfoot was a name to conjure with in 19th century Auckland. Lightfoots had been merchants when the main street was a slimy boardwalk and a rancid canal. Their enterprises survived war and slump and grew with the cutthroat frontier town. One disgusted colonial chronicler denounced the place as 'rotten to a degree & the inhabitants as a rule a lot of sharpers & thieves.' The scribe possibly had the Lightfoot clan in mind. The first years of the 20th century confirmed the family's mercenary flair. Wherever one looked there was a Lightfoot on show: not just in commerce, but in municipal affairs and national politics too. One Lightfoot was a two-term Auckland mayor; another was a cabinet minister of conservative colour. There were always faithful Lightfoot hands to be shaken when Britain's royals toured their furthest domain. (The family was never coy in looking after its own interests. In the New Zealand wars, largely fought about land, and the acquisition thereof, the Lightfoots had served with zest in the colonial militia and been rewarded with thousands of choice Maori acres.) The family was into its third generation of antipodean entrepreneurs when Rose Lightfoot was born in or about 1900, a late Victorian or early Edwardian. It is doubtful whether Rose ever interested herself in the how and why of her family's affluence. She was never a sophisticated girl. On the conventional view she was to be an even more unworldly woman.

It was as a lawyer that Alice had her first encounter with the Lightfoots. Alice had long been familiar with the name. Aside from the family's reputation as freebooting capitalists, the Lightfoots had for many years been clients of the legal firm in which Alice was a junior partner. Their sensitive affairs, however, were handled only by the firm's senior partners, men known for their discretion, distinctly never by the firm's rogue female.

That made it the more surprising, sometime in the middle 1930s, when a Mr Henry Lightfoot appeared in Alice's boxy office without warning. Perhaps his feeling was that such as Alice did not require prior appointment; that a lowly woman lawyer, unlike her male counterparts, should be on instant call. Alice was about to disillusion him in this respect, but finally thought better of a frosty rebuke. This Lightfoot was not, unlike most of his clan, conspicuously endowed with confidence in himself; he had a troubled and even tragic face. He was also, as it turned out, one of the lesser twigs of the Lightfoot tree: an unpretentious if able businessman who had never been in the forefront of his family's euphoric rush to riches.

'Do sit down, Mr Lightfoot,' she said, indicating her spare chair.

Henry Lightfoot did so with caution. For a time he found speech difficult; his mouth opened and closed soundlessly. Perhaps he was nonplussed by the novelty of finding himself in the hands of a capable woman. Alice may also have been even more intimidating than his expectation.

'I take it there is something I can help you with,' Alice finally said.

'Of a difficult nature,' Henry Lightfoot confessed.

'Which is what lawyers are for,' Alice pointed out.

'I wish to see you as more than a lawyer,' he explained.

'Oh? As what, then?'

'As a woman familiar with the larger world, perhaps.'

'As against what, Mr Lightfoot?' she asked.

'As against the narrow ways most women walk.'

'You flatter me, sir.'

'I think not. I imagine little surprises you.'

'Not overpoweringly,' Alice admitted. She couldn't see where the conversation was travelling. Shy Henry Lightfoot lifted his eyes to the ceiling. She waited until they found hers again.

'Are we to talk, then?' Alice inquired. Untypically, her tone was kind rather than curt.

Henry Lightfoot took a deep breath. 'I am here,' he said, 'to seek help and advice concerning my daughter. My daughter Rose.'

He was again in vocal difficulty.

'Please go on,' Alice urged gently.

'It is not,' Henry said, 'that Rose is a problem child. Quite the contrary. She is an extremely dutiful daughter. In almost every respect I have no complaint.'

'Nevertheless you feel need to see me on her account.'

Henry nodded. He explained, 'She suddenly fancies herself as a painter. An artist.'

'And isn't she?'

'The passion is there. It is not too much to say that she has been besotted with her paints and brushes since her mother died last year. She has little thought for anything else. What was formerly a ladylike hobby has now got out of hand. She now wants nothing more than to travel, to take tuition from distinguished names in the field, and above all to familiarise herself with masterpieces she can never see in this country.'

'I see nothing exceptional in that.'

'I see it ending badly,' Henry said.

'How so?'

'Rose is no longer young. She is a naive and middle-aged spinster. Europe, and the world of art, is full of traps for the unwary. Especially for a woman alone, a *moneyed* woman alone,' he added with lingering emphasis.

'So what do you wish of me in this connection?'

I am given to understand that you are knowledgeable in matters pertaining to art.'

'It is not a view widely shared,' Alice informed him. 'As a Sunday painter I have been damned with faint praise. Monday seldom fails to make me aware of my deficiencies.'

'In my connection that may be an advantage,' Henry assured her. 'Rose is altogether unaware of her shortcomings.'

'In your view, that is.'

'I freely admit that I am no authority on the subject.'

'Good,' Alice said. 'That may be helpful.'

'But I do see that any hope she entertains of a new life, a life in the arts, must be foolish in a woman nearing forty.'

'You leave me at a loss, sir. What is it you expect of me?'

'I should be grateful if you could bring a sympathetic eye to her situation. If you could likewise bring a dispassionate eye to her work, so much the better.'

'Am I,' Alice asked acidly, 'to understand that you wish your daughter hobbled? If so, you might consider the Chinese example. They bind the feet of female children soon after birth. I understand it is effective. They are too crippled to stray far from the kitchen. I fancy, however, that this procedure may be late in the day for your daughter.'

Henry struggled to hold his ground. 'I wish her given second thoughts, at least. Especially in respect of her worth as an artist.'

'That, I must say, Mr Lightfoot, is an original reason for consulting a lawyer.'

'I have nowhere else to turn,' he said. 'I have no artistic acquaintances. There has been no one in the family resembling Rose. And I do not wish to play stern and insensitive parent.'

Alice was quick to the point. 'And you wish me to?'

'I would not wish you to express any but your own view of her work.'

'As I would not, sir. Indeed my suspicion is that her work may not be the issue.'

Henry Lightfoot exhibited unease.

'Perhaps not altogether,' he confessed. 'My concern is that she is freed of the fancies which currently afflict her. Someone of authority and sympathy might best persuade her of the perils of her present course.'

'And you imagine I qualify?'

'Rose might be more comfortable with someone outside the family, especially with a woman of independent character.'

'Let us begin at the beginning,' Alice suggested.

'By all means,' Henry Lightfoot said.

Rose Lightfoot was an only child. Since her birth (a difficult one, which left her mother a longtime invalid) Rose had been the recipient of all the privileges a family of prosperous Aucklanders could bestow on a bright girl. There were expensive private schools. There were personal elocution teachers, piano teachers, singing teachers, and art teachers. There was everything to prepare the girl for an ornamental life in Auckland society.

Though she played the piano with competence, particularly for family guests, she was far more formidable alone at an easel. Sometimes she joined a group of well-mannered fellow artists on excursions into Auckland's outskirts: she painted picturesque landscapes and poignant Maoris. Were there young men on these excursions? If so, they were never mentioned. Auckland was distinctly short of acceptable young men after the First World War. Anyway her life was limited by the fact of her mother's indifferent health. So long as her mother lived there was no question of Rose leaving home to marry, not even much chance of her meeting up with a promising male. Her first duty was domestic. Without Rose the household would have come to a standstill. It was she who instructed servants in their tasks; who advised nurses in the care of her mother; who brushed lint from the shoulders of her father's suits before he went to his office. Her other pursuits were frivolous, or seen so by Lightfoot relatives. Homely Rose seldom required consideration; she was never much noticed at family festivities, seldom even congratulated on her musical and culinary contributions to such functions. Her virtue was taken for granted, and her practical nature. Her efficiency helped her parents survive the great depression of the 1930s, an event which left many Lightfoots lamenting, and some bankrupt. She continued to serve her parents diligently: she took in pupils of pianoforte and painting to help maintain her parents in monetary health.

Domestic servitude finished with her mother's death and the depression's end. Rose almost overnight began communicating impatience with her colourless existence; she made it evident that she now wished to live a life of her own. She had much to catch up on. Her urgent requirement was a grand tour of Europe. Her unencumbered contemporaries, and most of her young Lightfoot relatives, had made their European safaris years earlier. Most returned to become unexceptional husbands, wives and parents. Rose, however, wasn't looking for wedlock and childbirth or even a minor flutter. She assessed herself as no longer marriageable and probably beyond motherhood. Anyway marriage and motherhood interested her less than art. She wished to walk the great galleries of the Western world and wonder at its mighty museums and cathedrals. She wished to rifle art's secrets before age and infirmity made such a search impossible. Not only that. She now had means to do so, with an impressive legacy from her grateful mother. Large among Henry's concerns was the fear that it might be carelessly squandered. In that respect he was a routine Lightfoot after all.

Rose, as Alice recalled her thirty years later, was a tall, lean, straight-backed woman: her hair was short and crinkly, her lips thin. Potentially it was a severe face. It was certainly austere. She did not smile easily. Alice found it difficult to put her at ease on their first meeting. This took place in Rose's studio. It was a bright, airy loft with tall windows and a panoramic view of city and harbour. Her mother's money meant no expense had been spared in perfecting her environment; possibly no New Zealand artist of the time, amateur or professional, had a better appointed base. The walls swarmed with paintings old and new, the sum of two decades at her easel. In her artist's smock and Parisian beret, Rose confirmed the professional atmosphere of the place. There was only one thing wrong. It was too well-groomed by far. The anarchy of the outside world was hardly a whisper. If there was a delinquent spot of paint on the floor, Alice failed to see it. Shelves were not cluttered. There were no twisted tubes of paint visible, no crumpled drawing paper. Even the smell of turpentine was faint. Rose herself had surprisingly unsoiled hands. As a painter she remained an irreproachable housekeeper. For the most part her work also left the world shipshape. Her subject matter was unsurprising, much of it within walking distance of the family home. Most of her painting reflected the city's marine environment: sailing ships moored at the Auckland waterfront; children sporting at the sea's edge; Maoris gathering shellfish from Waitemata mudbanks; yachts leaning into the wind. Her earlier adventures as an art student — those weekends when she giddily escaped domestic responsibilities — were on record too. Here were logging teams carrying away the trimmed carcasses of kauri trees; there were Maori villages and pipe-smoking old women with tribal tattoos inscribed on their chins. Elsewhere were landscapes featuring Auckland's extinct volcanic cones and sometimes wide rivers, misty lakes and rugged coast. As an observer of the world, Rose was seldom half-hearted; her slant on her surroundings had something in common with a prisoner struggling to glimpse sky and bird beyond brick and bars. Above all the paintings spoke of a woman attempting to make the most of the little she knew of her land and its inhabitants. She was not greatly out of step with her New Zealand contemporaries. By cosmopolitan measure they were likewise decades behind the times. The shock wave of Paris's post-impressionist exhibition of 1910 had been a barely a ripple by the time it reached the antipodes. Rose's teachers, as arbiters of the acceptable, had done their work well. Landseer and Constable might have seen merit in her work. On her wall, in old English script, was the following programme:

Have genuine feeling to express.

Study the world attentively so that it can be expressed truthfully.

Find affinity with all that is most heartfelt in art.

Make it a duty to find beauty.

Never serve yourself selfishly, but attend art humbly, in whatever form that may take.

Ever be the handmaiden of art.

Alice was reluctant to determine how Rose's paintings measured up to this inspirational programme. She had already decided that the worth of the work was outside her brief. Yet something resembling talent *was* on show. Despite herself, Alice often looked twice and sometimes long and hard. Rose Lightfoot may have been deficient in some respects, but she had an enviable sense of colour; she knew what she was doing when she took up a brush and allowed the fall of light to firm her hand. Her draughtsmanship — or must we now say draughtspersonship? — was often impeccable.

So much for the paintings. Rose was a more difficult proposition.

'You are here on behalf of my father,' she said nervously.

'For you as much as he,' Alice claimed.

'Nevertheless, you would not be here were it not for him.'

It was pointless to deny it. 'His concern is for you alone and exposed in the world. As parents will, he fears the worst.'

'There is more,' Rose said.

'Of course. Naturally he wishes his daughter, his only child, near at hand. That, however, is not the beginning and end of it. His motive is not entirely selfish. He needs to know that what you want is worth the risk. That your ambition will not end in sorrow.'

'He frets that I am not good enough?'

'Perhaps,' Alice had to admit.

'I promise to bring him no grief,' Rose said.

'I am sure he means no distress either,' Alice replied.

So it went. After another such meeting, with Rose more relaxed, Alice reported to Henry. 'I have only two things to say,' she told him. 'First, your daughter is a determined girl. She feels, fairly enough, that she has missed out on too much. All she now asks is one bite at the apple.'

'Apple?' Henry said. 'What apple?'

'Perhaps that which ripened in Eve's garden.'

'And we know how that ended,' he said.

Alice shrugged. 'There is no Adam in the picture and, at this juncture, unlikely to be.'

'She is a plain girl,' Henry acknowledged.

'And a prudent one,' Alice pointed out. 'Besides, all we are talking about is a small and conventional European adventure. I cannot imagine her putting herself at risk. On the contrary, I imagine her likely to be too cautious for her own good.'

Henry thought on this, though with reluctance.

'You said you had two things to tell me,' he reminded her.

'The second concerns her work. Her painting.'

'Ah,' Henry said, with hope. 'What is your view?'

'That it is not to be dismissed. Whatever it may or may not be, it keeps her together. As for possible disappointments, we are familiar with those. They are not exclusive to those who think to serve the muses.'

This judgement was not good news to Henry either.

'So what are you saying?' he asked, though it should have been plain.

'Let your daughter go, Mr Lightfoot,' Alice said.

'Otherwise?'

'She will go anyway. If she leaves amicably, she may well be back sooner rather than later. If she leaves less than cordially, she may prolong her absence to prove a point to a possessive parent. If you wish a prediction, I think she could well find the larger world inhospitable — certainly for an unsophisticated and middle-aged New Zealand woman in breathless and belated pursuit of inspiration.'

'So what am I to tell her?' Henry asked helplessly.

'I imagined it obvious,' Alice answered.

At this point, in the dusk of a day many years later, Alice halted her narrative, and announced her need for a large gin and tonic. 'Is that wise?' I asked. We had just emptied a formidable bottle of red from Alice's favoured Dalmatian vineyard.

'Do you want to hear the rest,' she asked, 'or do you not?'

I fetched the gin fast.

'There is something to be said for age,' Alice announced.

'My hearing must be all to hell. I haven't heard you saying it.'

She ignored me.

'As the years pass,' she persisted, 'I find I have less on my conscience. Lovers cruelly banished and husbands deceitfully treated have become an unholy jumble. Sometimes I fail to recall their faces. Rose Lightfoot, however, remains difficult to dislodge.'

That surprised me. 'Rose? On your conscience?'

'Along with her father. It may have been my worst week's work.'

'Come, now. This is extravagant, even from you. What else could you have said?'

'Anything but what I did say.'

'Why?'

'Not that it will come as a surprise, but she never became what she wished to be.'

I was puzzled. 'She didn't go to Europe?'

'She did. She did indeed.'

'What went wrong, then? Was she overwhelmed by what she found? Diminished too?'

'She was certainly overwhelmed,' Alice said. 'Diminished? Who is to say?'

'You,' I suggested.

Rose Lightfoot sailed for Europe in 1937. It was not the happiest of years for the human race, with worse in the making. People were perishing by the tens of thousands in Spain's civil war and Russia's lethal purges. Even more were filling graves in Ethiopia and China. It is possible that Rose never noticed. Even if she had, she would probably not have allowed war's lengthening shadow to dim her first year of liberation.

Her first stop was London, a small residential hotel just off Hampstead Heath. Everything was novel, everything thrilling, to this once subdued New Zealand woman. No matter how damp the day, how uncomfortable the temperature, Rose was out sketching, painting, and wandering through churches and galleries. It seemed that friends and family underestimated Rose. Relatives who glimpsed her in London marvelled at her sudden self-sufficiency as she dashed with gusto from location to location, revelling in all that city offered. She was, it seemed, no wallflower in the wide world. Her step was brisk; her expression no longer hangdog. They — her relatives — were at a loss to explain this. They saw only a solo woman. They weren't to know that Rose was revelling in the company of friends. Deceased most of her accomplices might be, but their mastery of brush and paint was deathless. She didn't talk of a return home; she tended to look baffled when the subject was raised.

Alice was among the many favoured with Rose's passionately scribbled postcards. Her handwriting became even more illegible with excitement after she boarded a boat for France. Paris was all that legend promised. After surveying the Louvre, and scrupulously recording her likes and dislikes, she hurtled on to Nice and a small hotel off the Promenade des Anglais. It was, or so her messages signalled, bewitchingly cosmopolitan. Among other guests were an Italian count and a Romanian composer. There were also more commonplace folk from Holland, Sweden and England. One of the latter, a short, brisk and busty Scotswoman — a freelance journalist of sorts and going under the mannish name of Mac — took Rose under her wing. Rose was clearly fascinated by Mac; she was mentioned more and more in her letters. Mac cropped her hair short, wore slacks, smoked small cigars, and as a seasoned traveller made herself understood fluently in French and Italian. Aside from her brief involvement with Alice, it was Rose's first experience of a liberated woman and certainly her first of a wholly cosmopolitan one. Did it suggest one direction she might take? Had Henry Lightfoot been around, he might have been dismayed by the racy company his daughter was keeping; Alice herself might have been surprised. The fact is, however, that Mac steered Rose past the commonplace pitfalls of travel. She also took Rose to places which she might never have visited alone: to casinos, to opera, to concerts. They travelled together to Monaco and Cannes and then, more widely, through Genoa, Pisa and Florence, including a side trip into Serbia with its vivid little villages, cobbled streets and ancient inns. Her letters grew even more effervescent as her pen and brush became busy. Mac remained the liveliest and most considerate of friends. Did she have designs on Rose? If so, they were not manifest and not necessarily Sapphic. With her overflowing purse, her power to spend freely, the New Zealander must have made a desirable travelling companion for a relatively impecunious freelance writer. This is not to say that Mac was heartlessly free-loading on Rose. Rose would have insisted on paying the bills, and Mac's companionship would have seemed cheap at any price. In that respect Rose was never in hazard. Risk, if it was, resided elsewhere. It whispered through the cathedrals and galleries which left Rose dizzy. It dwelt in the insurrectionary first commandment of art: Thou shalt know no other God.

The couple meant to make Venice — where else? — the centrepiece of their journey. This had been Rose's hope all along. If her grail was anywhere, it had to be Venice. She had already arranged a longer stay there than elsewhere. With an experienced traveller at her side Venice was bound to be even more enriching.

Then, just short of Venice, Mac called a stop. Her father was ill; an editor was demanding promised travel articles. Anyway she had to race home. This was shattering. Rose's first inclination was to return to London with Mac.

'You mustn't dream of it,' Mac protested. 'Fancy travelling all this distance and not seeing Venice. It is inconceivable.'

Privately Rose found it unthinkable too. She had been in love with Venice — or with an imagined Venice — for most of her life. She had re-read all three volumes of Ruskin's *The Stones of Venice* in preparation for the day she saw the city. Mac was right. Even at the risk of losing so dear and helpful a friend, Rose couldn't turn back now. Nor did she.

Rose's letters and postcards to New Zealand continued to suggest that homecoming was far from imminent. It was never referred to. As months passed this omission became more and more perceptible.

'So what do you make of it?' Henry asked.

'An affair,' Alice suggested playfully, and immediately regretted it. Henry was not a man to be teased. His daughter was everything.

'With Europe, of course,' she added quickly.

Henry's sigh was heartfelt.

'And that is all?' he asked.

'Insofar as I can interpret her postcards.'

'I cannot help feeling that there might be more to them than meets the eye.'

Alice couldn't bring herself to disagree.

What didn't meet Henry's eye, and was vague even to Alice, was that Rose wished the year never to end. In a very real sense she was to be granted that wish. She arrived in Venice in mid- autumn and, still buoyed by exhilaration, surprised by her mounting competence as a traveller, immediately determined to remain there, if not forever, then at least far longer than her original itinerary prescribed. She moved into the Pensione Doge on the edge of the Piazza San Marco. Her balcony overlooked the pigeon-clouded square and the Doge's Palace, with bewitching glimmers of lagoon beyond. Her journal entries became rapturous. 'A most perfect Venetian day,' she said in an early postcard. 'Such soft pastel colouring. Such exquisite reflections. *Romantica! Poetica!*'

Half sea, half land, it seemed a city which drank in light. The lines of a hundred literary travellers kept coming to her lips. ('Ocean's nursling,' said Shelley. 'Enthroned on a hundred islands,' said Byron.) No painting, no tinted photograph, had prepared her for this salad of sights. The autumnal light continued to thrill her. Buildings were misty and the pigeons muted. The last of the year's pilgrims were padding across the Bridge of Sighs or gliding along the canals in uncomfortably moist gondolas. There was still warmth enough for open-air cafes fringing the Piazza San Marco to be pleasant. In the Cafe Lavena Rose filled her daily quota of postcards and letters, brought her journal up to date, and took coffee from an indolent waiter. It would have been easy to mistake her as merely another middle-aged woman poignantly prolonging a once-in-a-lifetime tour: as a woman waiting for something which would never quite happen. An observer might have been surprised to learn that Rose was convinced that her veins were filling with fate. She knew she had been born to walk Venice. Sometimes she sketched. Her eyes were never empty. Her ears were as alert. She revelled in the conversation at neighbouring tables.

Among regulars in the Lavena was a larky group of young men with no apparent means of support but always magically in money. Mixed in nationality, with several languages at their command, they talked art and literature in loud voices, as though attempting to attract eavesdroppers. They seldom failed to. They left the impression that they were writers and painters, and a few in fact were. By far the most conspicuous in the group was a willowy young man the others called Pierre. Laughter came easily to elegant Pierre Lacroix. He had cupid lips and wavy hair and wore white suits which emphasised his slender silhouette. It was easy to imagine him party to numerous amorous escapades. Did Rose imagine him so? Possibly. On the whole, however, Pierre remained in the realm of the unthinkable. Though she wasn't to know it, and might well have been shocked, he and his companions were of the genially predatory kind often found in the watering holes of Europe's wealthy. This roving band lived by filling romantic need; they gave satisfaction. They especially entranced spinsters and widows. They weren't cheap gigolos or, for that matter, saturnine adventurers on the prowl. Their services were not significantly sexual; many were effeminate anyway. For their clients it was sufficient that their escorts were personable, graceful and fluent.

Uppermost in the minds of Pierre and his companions, in this season, was a warm winter billet. It was time for hired gallants to hibernate. Rose's appearance in their cafe was therefore providential. Pierre — who else? — was first to the charge.

One morning, at breakfast, Rose found him standing by her table. 'Madam is alone here?' he asked in an unidentifiable accent.

'I am,' Rose agreed.

'Then perhaps madam might care to share her table?' he proposed.

'Of course,' she answered warmly. She might have pointed out that there were chairs vacant at other tables, entire tables free. She never faintly considered saying so.

By breakfast's end they knew all that was essential about each other. By lunch they knew much that wasn't. Pierre's friends, congregated over coffee and cognac in a far corner of the cafe, endeavoured not to look on, but naturally did. There were smiles and sometimes light laughter. Finally they drifted off and left their comrade to his masterful lady-killing.

His first line had been classic.

'I am a poet,' he informed Rose.

She nodded earnestly, worried that she might not have heard right. She had, and was won. What else could he have been? She had never seen him without a notebook under his arm; she had also observed him assiduously scribbling when not in company.

'You?' he asked.

'A painter,' she confessed.

'So,' he said.

'So,' she agreed shyly.

'Perhaps we were made to meet in Venice.'

Women, in his experience, found this thought compelling. It proved so again. Rose found it difficult to free her eyes from his earnest gaze.

There were more confidences. He was the son of a French-Canadian businessman and an aristocratic Spanish beauty and had spent his first years shuttling between Madrid and Montreal. In keeping with her family custom, his Anglophile mother pushed him into an English public school. This led to quarrels, and finally a break with his parents. 'It was never my wish to be an English gentleman,' he explained wryly. 'It was never their wish that I should be a poet.' His ancestral medley explained his distinctive accent. Though equally at home with Spanish and French, he now wrote, or tried to write, in English.

'It is not always easy,' he added. 'Sometimes I think it is good. Sometimes I fear not.'

'If it is a question of language, perhaps I might be of assistance,' Rose said.

'You?' he said, seemingly astonished.

'Of course,' she insisted.

'What can I say?' he said, with a warming smile. 'You do me much honour.'

'Perhaps you can dine with me tonight,' Rose said daringly. 'Perhaps we can talk of your poetry then.'

'Madam is kind,' he said.

'Call me Rose,' she said.

'Rose,' he smiled. 'That is charming.'

'And while I think to mention it,' she said, 'your shirt is a little grubby. You must give it to me. It will be clean tomorrow. You are also about to lose a button from your left sleeve; it needs needle and thread.'

By way of gratitude, Pierre came up with another reliable line.

'Did you know,' he asked, 'that Venice has seven hundred churches and four hundred bridges?'

Rose did, of course. To say so, however, might interrupt his flow. 'So many?' she said with feigned incredulity.

'You will see them all,' he promised. 'The large and the small, especially those with hidden delights.'

Some delights were not particularly clandestine. Two days later Pierre Lacroix moved into Rose Lightfoot's pensione. From that day forward he never lacked a clean shirt or lost a button. His room, next to hers, shared her balcony. In the afternoons Pierre and Rose were to be seen conferring over poems fresh from his pen at their favoured table at the Lavena.

The mechanics of verse, it soon appeared, interested Pierre rather more than its meaning. 'My last major work experimented with the symmetrical structure of Dante's *Divine Comedy*,' he explained passionately. 'My next, which I shall title *The House of Orseoli*, is to be even more ambitious. A narrative poem in fifteen cantos, it will tell the story of the dynasty of 10th century Venetian doges who made the city great.'

How could Rose not be impressed? Pierre went on, 'I shall employ six-line stanzas with unrhymed tetrameter in the middle. The task may be beyond me, but I would not forgive myself if I failed to try. Do you not feel the same about your work?'

'Often,' Rose assured him truthfully.

'Then we are of a kind,' he announced. Soon Rose was copying out his six-line stanzas (with unrhymed tetrameter in the middle) in an immaculate script. Capital letters, when they led off a stanza, were lovingly illuminated in medieval manner. Pierre's former cronies were tactful; they never invited themselves to the table where Rose and Pierre sat in something like trance. Most were moving on anyway, often with envious glances in the direction of their fortunate colleague. Pierre seemed safe for the winter. They weren't to know that they had seen the last of him, though Pierre himself might have suspected as much. At thirty, after a decade of noisy cafes and dilatory liaisons, Pierre had begun to weary of the nomadic life. His was no seasonal tryst.

Alice sighed. The level of her gin and tonic was sinking. 'Naturally we had no idea of this at the time,' she explained. 'There were no preliminaries. No hints. Nothing to prepare us at all. Then, out of nowhere, Rose reported that she had acquired a Spanish nobleman — a man, moreover, whom she meant to marry. Henry Lightfoot and I received letters to that effect on the same day. Overwrought Henry was in my office within an hour of receiving his. He had only the one thought — that Rose had been ensnared by some damnable dago fortune hunter. He put it even more fiercely than that when he learned that the said aristocrat had literary leanings. "A bloody pansy poet too," he said in despair.'

Henry had only a day or two to decide how best to rescue his daughter. A quick steamer trip to Europe seemed in order. Then further letters arrived. These brought the news that the pair had married in Venice with assistance from the British consul and an Anglican cleric. Though a Roman Catholic, Pierre had consented to marry in a Protestant church.

'*Consented*?' Henry said, just short of apoplexy.

'Consented,' Alice said calmly.

'I hope I never meet this Senor High and Mighty in an alley on a dark night,' Henry said.

Rose said that the ceremony had been simple. 'Very sweet and beautiful,' she reported. 'Just as the wedding of a poet and his muse should be.'

That was the first hint that Rose had found her life's calling. The fait accompli all but finished Henry. The swiftest steamer was of no use now. His daughter was lost. It was worse than his bleakest expectation. A Spanish nobleman? A poofter poet? Dear God. The Lightfoots could be the laugh of Auckland. '"I should be grateful if you didn't mention it," Henry said to me.'

There was a honeymoon. The newlyweds purchased a car and travelled down to Greece and finally back to Venice. Though she didn't say so, Rose felt this superfluous. She needed no further holiday from life. Venice was idyll enough, Venice and Pierre.

'What now?' she asked on their return. She imagined them

renting an old palace on a quiet canal, desirably within easy walk of the Lavena, where Pierre could arrange rhyme schemes to his satisfaction.

'London,' he announced.

'London?'

'Most definitely, I think. Perhaps we might live there for a time. All things say that it is time to publish. I cannot hide myself in Venice forever.'

Rose hid her dismay. 'Since you put it like that,' she said.

'There is no other way to put it,' he assured her.

In London, Rose and Pierre settled into a small Bloomsbury hotel. The British Museum was around the corner. Pierre researched and wrote in the museum's famous round room. Rose remained in their hotel, conscientiously continuing to copy and embellish Pierre's manuscripts. What did she think of his verse? We need only know that she treated it with reverence. The fact is that outside the romantics — outside Wordsworth and Keats, Byron and Shelley, and especially Shelley, Pierre was not widely read in English literature. His one surviving prose work, it might be noted, was titled *Shelley, Lyre and Lance*. It suggested that he was something more than a dazzled worshipper of the long-dead poet; it remarkably implied that he *was* Shelley, perhaps even destined, like his distinguished antecedent, to disappear in dangerously deep water. Certainly, in his verse narrative *A Promethean Trilogy*, he demonstrated that he was not shy about picking up where Shelley left off.

Raised on Palgrave's *Golden Treasury*, Rose was no more familiar with literature's current concerns than her husband. Neither noticed that the republic of letters, after insurrection and coup d'état, was now flying a flag of a different colour. They were decades out of touch. For Pierre as much as Rose, Eliot and Pound had proselytised in vain. Even the plain speech of Hardy and Frost was unromantically modern. Such contemporaries did not serve beauty. Rose refused despair as one English editor after another coolly declined to publish Pierre's work. Rose was not a woman to lose faith easily. Not in Pierre; not in beauty's truth. Scores of much-thumbed books had told her that true genius was misjudged in its own time. Her mission was to see that this was not her husband's fate.

Though they rang with Pierre's virtues, her letters and postcards did not speak of an early return home with her exotic husband. Henry found these communications excruciatingly short of personal detail. It was as if Pierre was the point of her existence; that she had no other life. What of hers?

'At least she sounds happy,' Alice ventured.

Henry had no view on the subject.

In fact the two were short on bliss. The English winter was bitter. London was dank, grey and cramped. Pierre's disgust with the place, and its cruelly exclusive literary fraternity, mounted daily. Rejection, despite Rose's best efforts, remained his lot. In an attempt to turn his tide of complaint she looked up her friend Mac; perhaps Mac had literary friends who might help Pierre into print. At the least Mac, a professional who contributed to the literary pages of Sunday papers, might have some amiable advice. Mac had, but it was short of amiable. Rose learned that friendships formed with fellow wayfarers frequently fail to survive journey's end. For one thing confidences are easier to share with peripatetic strangers. On home ground Mac was brisker than Rose recalled; and impatient with Rose's news of her life. She was unimpressed by the company Rose was keeping. And especially by what she heard of Pierre.

'It sounds as if you have fallen in with cultural lumpens,' she observed.

'Lumpens?' Rose asked.

'Or poseurs,' Mac said. 'In either case worthless.'

She examined Pierre's bundle of manuscripts in offhand fashion. She didn't sigh, but her expression was pained. Finally she pushed the poems aside.

'What can I say?' she asked.

Rose leaned forward attentively.

'They are extremely pretty,' Rose went on.

There was only Mac's astringent tone to suggest that this was not necessarily a blessing.

She went on, 'It grieves me to say it, but your splendid calligraphy and exquisite illuminations are quite wasted on this metrical mush.'

Rose tried to grasp this, and failed.

'You wish my advice to your young man?'

'My husband,' Rose was quick to say.

Mac winced, if not conspicuously. 'Tell him to get a useful job,' she said.

That might have sounded final. It was not.

'A useful job?' Rose heard herself say, indignant and breathless.

'You tell me that he has Spanish blood,' Mac went on. 'If so, he should make himself useful with a rifle in Spain. That is where the real poetry of our time is being written. The ranks of the International Brigade are rich in writers fighting fascism. Shelley would have been there. Byron too. Any poet worth his salt is now.'

Rose had forgotten that Mac was a Communist Party member, not only writing for the *The Daily Worker* but selling it outside tube stations too. Until now this had seemed an unimportant and endearing idiosyncrasy.

'On the other hand,' Mac mused, 'his alleged aristocratic background, and his landed connections, suggest that he might be shot as a fascist. I am sorry to be brutal, but these are brutal times.'

Rose needed no further convincing on that score. She made awkwardly for the door, Pierre's manuscripts under her arm.

Mac moved to hold the door open. This time her voice wasn't unkind. 'Poor Rose,' she said. 'How I wish that I had gone with you to Venice. You would certainly not be out of your depth.' She reached out gently; her hand rested briefly on the younger woman's face. Rose flinched. What was Mac saying? That she, Rose, might be better off without Pierre? She loyally decided not to think further on the subject.

Compassionately, perhaps moved by Rose's expression, Mac added, 'If you mean to persist in peddling this young man's poems, let me give you a word of advice. A publisher isn't necessary. A printer is. All that is necessary is money. There are printers who specialise in producing volumes subsidised by the author, particularly by poets desperate to see themselves in print. Though now rather frowned on, the practice was once commonplace. These days such printers are known as vanity publishers.'

'Vanity publishers?' Rose said uneasily. 'Pierre is not conceited.'

'Name a poet who wasn't,' Mac said cheerfully. 'Meanwhile bless you, dear, and good luck.'

They parted with promises to keep in touch. Even as these were uttered they knew they wouldn't. Their encounter, however, had a surprising consequence. Rose rid herself of paints and brushes, retaining only the pens and coloured inks she needed to serve Pierre's verse. She was nailing her colours to the mast, so to speak. She may also have been recalling one of the dictums conspicuous in her New Zealand studio: **Never serve yourself selfishly, but attend art humbly**. And, **Ever be the handmaiden of art**. She decided she had been a less than humble handmaiden. Between one day and the next Pierre became her life's work.

Mac's advice — if not in respect of Pierre embracing a rifle — proved helpful after all. Rose now knew how to get Pierre into print. The sooner he won the acknowledgement he needed from London, the faster they might be back in Venice. In this instance, and perhaps this instance only, she was selfish. Venice was the one place, the first place, where she felt free.

She found an agreeable printer, and paid to have Pierre's poems printed in a numbered edition of forty signed by the poet and with hand-coloured illustrations by his wife. Prophetically titled *Sorrows of the Hopeful,* the publication did not turn the literary world around. On the other hand it did no one harm. Ten were sent out for review and not heard from again. The couple began tripping over the thirty remaining.

In depression, Pierre found it easy to believe that London's literary cabal had conspired successfully to shut him out. He also suspected Jews, Bolshevists and Freemasons. He found it impossible to resume work on his classical drama *Pyramus and Thisbe*. He no longer read and researched in the museum reading room.

'Literature is dead and buried in this land,' he announced.

'Are you thinking of Venice again?' she asked.

'Perhaps Nice,' he said.

Rose was disappointed. 'Why not Venice?'

'It is of the past,' he explained.

'The past?' Rose said in dismay. Venice of the past? How could he think it? They had met there. They had wed there. It was their city.

'Is it me you wish,' he asked, 'or Venice?'

There was only one answer. She was silent.

He went on, 'Old friends now think Nice the better place to be. It is safer, they say. It is also French. Venice might soon be difficult for foreigners if Hitler and Mussolini push for war.'

This did not seem a genuine explanation, but then Rose seldom saw newspapers. She knew little of Hitler and not much more of Mussolini. And what was this about old friends? Why should he be feeling the need of them again? Had she begun to bore him? Was she about to lose him?

She wasn't. Pierre, for one thing, had no intention of mislaying her. He was never bored by money, nor with what it could buy. Currently it bought superb food, fine wine, and soft beds. It also provided first class fares to Nice.

Pierre was soon weaving among cafe tables again, seldom without an expensive cigarette between his slim fingers. He seemed years younger as old friends surrounded him. His smile was as winning as ever Rose had seen it; the eyes of both men and women lit up in response. Gone was the misery of London. He was in his world. He even announced a return to poetry.

'My muse calls again,' he said with a warm wink at Rose.

She felt a shiver of pleasure. It was what she most wished to hear. Her place in the world had never felt more solid.

Summer in Nice was a delight after winter in London. Pierre was working again on *Pyramus and Thisbe*. 'It may be my masterpiece,' he warned Rose. 'Perhaps they are born again in us.'

'Pyramus and Thisbe were doomed lovers,' Rose pointed out.

'Then we shall be careful,' Pierre said.

Lacking larger enterprises, Rose began transcribing his working journals, letters and notebooks.

'What are you doing with those?' Pierre asked.

'Making them readable,' Rose explained. 'Your handwriting is a fright. How anyone in the future will penetrate it, I cannot imagine. You should have respect for posterity.'

'I never think posterity,' he said playfully.

'What do you think, then?'

'Eternity,' he smiled.

The cafes of Nice began losing their frivolous character. By the time Rose and Pierre noticed, menace was almost upon them. They were obliged to observe that young men were disappearing from the seafront; that waiters were fewer and hotels emptying. Almost overnight half the males in France were in uniform. Disaster had begun pushing its cloud across the French Maginot Line.

'It is time to leave,' Pierre decided, a week later than wise.

They paid bills, packed bags and vainly looked for a taxi. Finally Rose and her Spanish grandee finished up running inelegantly to the nearest railway station, weighed down by suitcases, and fighting for standing room on a Paris-bound train. Paris did not feel safe either. Poland had just been invaded. After days of apprehension Britain and France were formally at war with Germany. Rose and Pierre blundered along half-dark streets in search of transport. At one point, tired of battling surly taxi-drivers, and winning contradictory directions from excitable Parisians, they found themselves in a lane in the Latin Quarter, sitting fatigued on their suitcases outside a small gallery dedicated to the tourist market. (It would soon be serving men of Hitler's legions in search of Parisian souvenirs.) The display window was still faintly lit. Along with cheap knick-knacks there were reproductions of Matisse and Renoir on sale. Conspicuous too was a scaled down replica of Rodin's The Kiss. Even in reduced form the robust sculpture retained its power.

'Look at that,' Pierre said. 'They are still embracing in a world gone mad.'

'Perhaps there is a poem in it,' Rose suggested.

'There is certainly a message,' Pierre said. He gazed at the sculpture silently and lit a cigarette. Despite a distant siren, he was in recognisably lyrical mood.

'What is it you see?' she asked.

'Love's triumph,' he explained.

Rose was moved. 'We must remember this moment,' she decided.

'Of course,' he said.

'Say forever,' she begged. 'Say as long as they kiss.'

'Forever,' he pledged. 'So long as love triumphs.'

At least they triumphed over the French transport system. They found a crowded train to the coast, and then a ferry to Dover, war at their heels. Then it was London again, and despair. It was even more unwelcoming than before. Though the war was being called phoney, people were seldom without gas masks. Barrage balloons, designed to entangle hostile aircraft, bulked in the sky. City-wide blackouts were becoming familiar too. Pierre and Rose concluded that there was no safety in Europe. Lines of escape were limited to two, leading to Canada or New Zealand. Pierre had friends and relatives in Montreal; she had father and family in Auckland. 'New Zealand is too far,' he argued. A shorter journey meant that peril from U-boats was less.

'U-boats?' Rose said.

'Or German raiders,' he said.

For Rose the exhilaration of exile was gone. Venice, for one thing, was on the far side of the war. Even on this side, no land was easy of access. She discovered herself homesick for New Zealand. Montreal was no substitute. But it was to be home so long as war lasted.

Alice sighed. 'It is a mystery what she did with herself during those years,' she said. 'What does a novelist do with such a gap in the narrative?'

'Invent,' I said. 'Fiction is what it says it is.'

'You want me to fib?'

'No more than you have been,' I said.

'I have tried to use my imagination,' Alice said.

'Try harder,' I urged.

'Unhappiness grew apparent in her letters. My suspicion is that there was more to it than being trapped in Canada. Possibly Pierre ceased to be as attentive as he had been. Possibly he had a past in Montreal, a past of which Rose was unaware. Perhaps a woman friend from his pre-cafe years. Perhaps a wife, divorced or otherwise. I cannot rule out bigamy. Anyway Rose was desperate to get home to New Zealand. Pierre remained unenthusiastic. Though he still lacked nothing of a monetary nature, her wealth no longer bewitched him as it had hitherto. What he *did* lack, yet again, was an audience. He failed to impress the custodians of Canadian literature. The country's critics proved as indifferent as the English had been.

'Perhaps it was then that Rose began romancing, presenting him with a programme meant to rouse him from creative doldrums. The South Pacific, she argued, was still little touched by the poet's pen. It was all open to him, much as it had been to Gauguin's brush. A new country was what he needed. New Zealand was what he needed. The South Sea had legends which rivalled Europe's. The New Zealand Maori had lovers' tales beside which Pyramus and Thisbe seemed colourless. And that was not to speak of their majestic settings of such legends — spellbinding mountains, mighty seas, sweeping beaches, glaciers and even volcanoes. Those tales and legends were in wait for him. He had only to say the word.'

'And he said the word?'

'Once the war was over,' Alice said. 'It ended in the same month as Henry Lightfoot's life. To the last, Henry held to the hope that his straying daughter would come back to him. When she did, he was under a shrinking mound of clay in an Auckland cemetery. That was the end of her nine-year grand tour. Rose was home.'

'And Pierre?'

'He distinctly wasn't. He found Auckland even more provincial than Montreal. Worse, it was glumly British. He walked colonial streets in the centre of the city, looking for something resembling a familiar environment. If this was the South Sea, he was not impressed. Bookshops were few and the art gallery stuffed with Victorian dross. Food was foul, and mostly steak and chips. There was nothing fit to be called a cafe. The best he could come up with was a place where half-drinkable coffee was on sale. (Cognac, puritanically, was not.) The customers of this establishment — insolvent architects, threadbare artists, hangdog journalists posing as poets — were an indifferent substitute for friends now on the far side of the world; these antipodeans were, in Pierre's view, too earnest by far. They lacked style, he said. They lacked finesse. "Always they talk the great New Zealand novel," he mocked. "Always they vanish up the great New Zealand navel." Not that these people detained him for long. A spirited social climber, he used these acquaintances as stepping stones. An authentic bohemian — as distinct from a southern hemisphere counterfeit — was a novelty in New Zealand. Eventually he became something of a social lion. He was invited to respectable parties where his opinions were sought on art, literature and politics. If existentialism was what his hosts wanted, existentialism he gave them. If gossip of the great, he could provide a colourful account of his meetings with Picasso, his encounters with Cocteau. He talked plausibly on anything and everything. Rose shyly cried off when these invitations came. Dinner parties were never to her taste. His fancies may have embarrassed her.'

'I imagine you met him,' I said.

'One could hardly evade him. If not with Rose — on whom I called in respect of legal matters — then at dinner parties and musical evenings. He was a most charming fellow. And most attentive to the ladies. It was generally agreed that he was quite a prize. Otherwise, I regret to say, there was absolutely nothing to him. Pierre Lacroix was proof of the proverb that empty vessels make the most sound. His conversation was as hollow as his verse, if that was possible.

'On Henry's demise Rose had inherited the family home and had been enriched by another large legacy. Pierre not only knew which side his bread was buttered; he knew where the jam was too. To be fair, he may have felt a prisoner. With Rose he played at being a suburban householder in a street as quiet as any in the land. They had a pet cat. They had nicknames for the birds which fluttered around their property. They gardened to colourful effect. The house sat among shady trees and shimmering cataracts of flowers. In summer Pierre was often to be seen hose in hand, making sure their precious plants survived summer drought. This is not how we imagine poets; not as prosaic citizens. Pierre, in the end, may also have failed to picture himself in his new role. Yet he seems to have tried. With Rose's impassioned backing, he founded a literary magazine in which his own work invariably had pride of place. He still, however, failed to reconcile himself to his current calling. When visitors dropped in, they found Rose but seldom Pierre. For much of the week, sometimes all week, he shut himself up in a work room to the rear of the house. And here was the problem. In Venice or Nice he had always been able to rely on some cafe regular interrupting his work in friendly fashion and buying him a drink. Here there were no conversational friends bearing cognac. Thrown back on his own resources, he found the well dry. It had never been more than moist anyway. He survived six years in Auckland. Then something gave. Perhaps one morning he found it impossible to recognise the face he saw in the mirror. He disappeared between one day and the next, likewise half Rose's capital. With some deft fiscal surgery he transferred some of her investments into his personal bank account, from which it was swiftly uplifted. Then he was gone. I made a few inquiries but his trail ended on the Auckland waterfront. It seems he left New Zealand on a boat bound for Tahiti. That made sense; Tahiti's waterside cafes were a reasonable approximation of Europe's. Perhaps he found the time ripe to familiarise himself with Gauguin's haunts; perhaps he saw a sequence of poems in following the great painter's footsteps. Who is to say? He may still be an ageing beachcomber in Tahiti. On the other hand one seemingly reliable source says that he returned to Canada, remarried, and died there some years ago. Who knows? If memory serves right, he vanished in the year 1951. Rose was fifty-one years old. And alone.'

'And shattered, I imagine.'

Alice gave me a pained look. 'You have an extremely conventional turn of mind,' she said. 'For a novelist that is fatal.'

'Are you talking,' I protested, 'or just finding a stick to beat me with? How could she not have been devastated?'

'I am telling you that she declined to notice,' Alice said.

'Notice what?'

'Are you naturally dense, or do you just work hard at it? She declined to notice him gone.'

There was a silence; I refused to be irritated. Alice at last said, 'What are we doing tomorrow?'

'It's up to you,' I said. 'I thought a drive somewhere.'

'I also have one in mind,' she disclosed. 'One which might give you something to think about.'

'Are you going to tell me where, or must it be a mystery?'

'Until tomorrow,' she said.

'You haven't finished Rose's story,' I pointed out.

'You may have to,' she said. 'The years are against me. You'll see what I mean tomorrow.'

'Promise?'

'Promise,' she said. There was wile in her eye.

Next day, at breakfast, I tried to win a little more intelligence of the day's mission. 'I'd like to know where I'm going,' I protested. 'After all, I *am* your chauffeur.' Alice remained indifferent to this plea; she continued to be infuriating. We drove along the sunlit city seafront, the Waitemata harbour bright to our right. 'Turn left,' she ordered tersely as downtown Auckland drifted to our rear. 'Now right. That's it. Now left again.' We were soon travelling streets rich in wooden Victorian villas and bow-windowed Californian bungalows. It was a quiet and leafy quarter, with glimpses of sea beyond bulky trees: as pleasant a suburb as any in mid-century Auckland, and favoured by the city's professional class.

'This should do,' she decided.

I helped Alice from the car. Shaky, she leaned on her stick.

'So here we are,' she said.

'Here *you* are,' I said. 'Where am I?'

She had commanded me to halt outside the one dwelling in the street with a neglected appearance. With twin turret rooms, ornate verandahs and fluted woodwork, it had obviously once been one of the grander residences in the vicinity. It was now almost submerged in vegetation, in dishevelled hedge, tall weeds, and wild roses. Paint peeled from weatherboards, and the corrugated iron roof showed rust. Alice took a couple of steps toward a sagging picket gate set in the barricade of growth.

I failed to go with her. 'Wait,' I said.

'What is it?' she asked irritably.

'First you tell me what this is about.'

'Must I?' she sighed.

'You must,' I confirmed.

'I could become extremely bad-tempered,' she informed me.

'I could too,' I said. 'Do you want a very public fight?'

That gave her second thoughts. 'Very well,' she decided graciously. 'Though I remain sorely tempted, I daresay an ambush isn't fair.'

'What does that mean?'

'That I don't want you to lose your tongue. You are going to need it.'

'Oh?' I asked.

'You are about to meet Rose Lightfoot. Or Rose Lacroix, as she continues to call herself.'

I was shaken. To this point Rose had been wispily fictional and presumably deceased.

'She's still alive?'

'Why shouldn't she be?' Alice said stiffly. 'Aren't I?'

'All the same,' I said.

'All the same, nothing,' Alice said. 'Keep to the point. You are about to meet the heroine of our tale.'

'Your tale,' I said. 'Not mine.'

'It will be,' she predicted.

Thirty years on, too late to please her, it seems Alice has won.

Alice knocked on the door. There was no response. 'Not unusual,' Alice explained. 'She refused to hear the telephone when she had one. Then she saw it made life easier to have it disconnected.'

I was edgy. 'Then perhaps we should respect her privacy,' I suggested. 'I'm willing to take your word that she's still with us.'

'Coward,' Alice said.

She pushed a side door open and called Rose's name several

times. There was a shuffling sound somewhere within the house. It solidified into footsteps. 'Alice?' a voice asked. 'Is that you, Alice?'

'Here,' Alice called.

Rose Lightfoot surfaced from the shadowy interior. She was rather less dilapidated than I supposed. That Auckland day she was near her seventieth birthday, but not especially looking her age. Her hair might have been greying, but she still carried herself well. And she wasn't conspicuously feeble. In spite of her unstylish dress she retained a reasonable elegance.

She began ushering us indoors. 'And who have we here?' she asked, meaning me.

'My great-nephew,' Alice said.

'The literary one?'

'The same,' Alice agreed. 'He is staying a week or two with me.'

'That is a thrill for you both,' Rose suggested.

'I don't think *he* would call it enthralling,' Alice said. 'Who needs to be trapped with this grumpy relic for a fortnight?'

Rose looked at me with interest. 'You realise that your aunt never stops talking of you?'

'No,' I said.

'Nor does he need to know,' Alice said briskly.

'It's true,' Rose insisted.

'Do shut up, Rose,' Alice said.

We journeyed down a long passage to a large lounge. There were paintings from floor to ceiling and on every wall. They plainly belonged to the years before Venice and Pierre Lacroix. Interspersed with the paintings were framed photographs of a lean and rather lordly man who could only be Pierre. There must have been most of a hundred such photographs, large and small; there was nowhere to escape his faintly petulant spoiled-boy gaze.

There he was at a cafe table, a long drink before him, the Mediterranean beyond. There he was resting against a stone wall in Athens, the Acropolis to his rear. There he was with Rose, both dressed formally, on what must have been their wedding day. The settings changed. London was there, Nice, Monaco, Montreal, Auckland. And above all Venice. Their past swarmed around us. I was still taking it in when Rose spoke.

'Pierre, of course, will be delighted to see you,' she said.

'Pierre?' I said with wonder. I looked to Alice for rescue. She was no help. She appeared to be contemplating the ceiling.

'Pierre is my husband,' Rose explained. 'He is always lamenting the lack of genuine literary company in New Zealand.'

'Why should that be?' I asked.

'He is a poet,' she said.

I pretended astonishment. 'Really?'

'Didn't Alice tell you? I daresay you will make his day.'

Again I looked feebly to Alice. Again she refused to meet my eye. I felt a faint flutter in my spine. Either Alice had misled me, or Rose Lightfoot was mad. Or both women were.

'There is so much in Europe he still misses,' Rose went on. 'New Zealand's lonely mountains and empty shores are no compensation for what he has lost. But as I often tell him, you can't have everything.'

'No,' I said, still in difficulty.

'Now and then I worry that he may want to rove again. I point out that we are no longer young. And that the world — and especially Europe — is no longer as it was.'

'That is true,' I said judiciously.

'You must make a point of saying so to Pierre,' she said. 'I'm sure you will enjoy each other. It is a pity you aren't familiar with his verse.'

'Indeed,' I said.

'We can remedy that,' she announced. To Alice she said, 'Do you mind if I steal your engaging young relative away?'

'You would be doing me a favour,' Alice said. 'Don't feel obliged to bring him back.'

'Come,' Rose beckoned. 'This way.'

Alice moved tactfully to the kitchen while Rose led me further into the house. Enshrined on a sideboard, in the glow of a red lamp, were six highly polished and expensively crafted wooden boxes. Inlaid lettering announced that these boxes contained the collected poems of Pierre Lacroix volumes I to VI. In the manner of a conjuror Rose began lifting the lids of each to reveal bejewelled manuscripts resident in beds of blue velvet. There was a life's work in the fastidiously illuminated pages. 'Feel free to touch,' Rose said. 'I frequently make a point of doing so. I feel Pierre's music ripple through my fingertips.'

I didn't know where to begin.

'Pull up a chair,' she urged. 'Make yourself comfortable. I shall see what wickedness your great-aunt is up to in the kitchen.'

She left me and joined Alice. While the two women talked in low voices, I found a chair and obediently began picking a path through Pierre's poems. There was sonnet and sestina, rondeau and rondelet; there were classical dramas of a rococo kind. Though there was an occasionally attractive tinkle of nouns and adjectives, music failed to survive his tick-tocking stanzas. Most of the poems belonged to that species of literary construct Ezra Pound likened to the sonorous farting of a goose. It was an unkindness to trespass among them. Though I endeavoured to remain a conscientious browser, my eyes roamed away from the poems on the page to the paintings on the wall; there was no difficulty in deciding which were worth attention. Thus musing, I heard the sound of a whistling kettle. Then Alice called. Relief, in the form of morning tea, was on hand.

As I closed a last lid on Pierre Lacroix it struck me that the six boxes made six sumptuous coffins.

'So what do you think?' asked Rose as I rejoined the ladies.

'He has great bravura,' I replied. 'Rather remarkably in this day and age, he roves fearlessly through every verse form extant.'

'Most remain as vivid as the day he wrote them,' Rose said. 'I was only telling Pierre so last night.'

'Of their kind,' I agreed, 'they are most distinctive.'

Meanwhile I was thinking: Pierre? Last night?

'Good,' Rose said. 'Don't feel obliged to spend more time on them today, unless you must.'

'They certainly aren't to be read in a hurry,' I said.

'Indeed not,' she said.

'However,' I went on, rather fatally, 'I must say that your paintings are something of a distraction. Even with Pierre's poems before me,

I found it difficult to keep my eyes off them. Why have they been hidden?'

There was tension at the table. Alice yet again declined to meet my eye. Rose appeared to be looking at her empty hands. I was aware of a conversational blunder.

Finally Rose said, 'That is most flattering. If it is your intention to humour me, young man, you are under no such obligation.'

'Forgive me,' I said. 'Flattery was far from my mind.'

'You aren't saying that Pierre's work is less pleasing than mine?'

'Never,' I claimed hastily. 'In any case a poem cannot be equated with a painting. It is like comparing chalk with cheese. Affinities of that sort are best left to academics with too much time on their hands.'

Rose forgave me, or seemed to. Strain passed. 'Do you smoke?' she asked sociably.

'Alas,' I said.

'Please feel free. You might care to try one of Pierre's Turkish cigarettes. He has them on order from his old tobacconist in Nice.'

'I prefer my pipe,' I said apologetically.

'Come on,' she said. 'Just the one. They are cigarettes with a very friendly smell. I am always telling Pierre so.'

She fetched an ashtray and a carved Serbian cigarette box from the mantelpiece and placed them before me. The cigarettes were long and black, elegantly tipped with gold. 'Take more than one if you wish,' she said. 'Pierre won't mind in the least.'

'One will do,' I insisted.

After some fumbling, I managed to ignite one of the cigarettes. 'How is it?' she asked, a shade anxiously.

'Very friendly,' I assured her.

Rose turned to Alice. 'There is,' she said, 'no substitute for the familiar smell of a man's tobacco about the house.'

'On one view of the matter,' Alice said. 'On the other hand I can do without his wretched pipe.'

'But at least you know where to find him. I seldom have a problem locating Pierre. His scent beckons me.'

At that point I ruined Rose's accolade to tobacco by coughing and spluttering. As I anticipated, the cigarette was old and musty, a decade or two past its shelf-life. The highly inflammable tobacco scorched my tongue.

'Dear me,' Rose said.

A smile hovered on Alice's mouth.

'I am not,' I said, 'very good with cigarettes.'

'Never mind,' Rose said. 'Try another.'

'One is enough,' I protested.

'At least the fragrance is there,' Rose said, sniffing. 'It brings back many memories, mostly of when Pierre and I were young on the Grand Canal and the Promenade des Anglais.'

I was sure it did. I said nothing.

Alice had come with the ingredients of a civilised morning tea: cucumber sandwiches and pastries and cake were arranged on fragile plates. There was one curiosity, however. The table was set for four rather than three. And Alice poured tea into four cups. Entering into the spirit of the thing, I pretended not to see anything amiss as the fourth cup cooled without anyone reaching for it. As she sipped her own tea, Rose's gaze moved to an ornate mantel clock. Was she waiting on a fourth party to put in an appearance? It seemed so. Minutes must have passed before I realised that the hands of the clock were stationary. Possibly they hadn't moved for years; anyway the clock suggested that she had grown indifferent to time since Pierre sped off to Tahiti. Was she hoping for it to begin ticking magically, heralding the return of her husband? Or was she waiting, as promised, on forever? Without referring to me, my aged companions continued to make conversation. This allowed me to become less fidgety. The fact was, however, that their discourse made little sense, especially when it touched on Pierre. Most of Rose's contribution was laced with what he had lately said and done. It was altogether convincing. Had we been in a courtroom — with me a juror, Rose a witness — I should have believed every word. Alice gave me a sly, rather triumphant glance as she offered cake. It was no use looking to her for deliverance. At least not until she had her money's worth of my discomfort.

I must have survived an hour of incomprehension. Then Alice compassionately judged it time to leave. Rose's gaze travelled to the extinct clock again. 'I cannot imagine where Pierre is,' she said. 'I daresay he'll turn up, as usual, the minute you've gone.'

'I'm sure,' Alice said.

'And as for you, young man,' Rose added, 'please feel free to visit again. Nothing delights Pierre more than an encounter with a real writer. There are so few in this country, you know. Pierre can be most bitter about the mediocrities who preside over literary reputations here. Perhaps you could arrange a signed copy of one of your books. It would mean a great deal to Pierre to find a friend. Can you?'

'Of course,' I promised.

'I'll see he doesn't forget,' Alice said.

Then I was out in the street with Alice. Rose Lacroix didn't accompany us into the light. She saw us off from the dim front hall of her house. I suspected that she hadn't gone beyond it in years.

We drove away. 'Well,' I sighed.

'Indeed,' Alice said. 'You behaved satisfactorily, considering.'

'What is that supposed to mean?' I asked.

'Considering your faux pas.'

'About her paintings?'

'Exactly.'

'It was innocent enough,' I protested. 'And her paintings breathe more than his poems.'

'Nevertheless it was heartless. You were stripping her life of its point.'

'Meaning Pierre?'

'Who else?'

'I begin to see,' I confessed.

'Not before time,' Alice said.

For ten minutes or more, as I negotiated central Auckland, we had nothing to say.

Finally Alice said, 'You won't forget that book, will you?'

'That would be difficult,' I said. 'Signing a book for a versifier's shade will be a novel experience, in both senses of novel.'

'As usual, you are missing the point,' Alice informed me. 'If you have taken in anything, over the past hour, it is surely that Pierre Lacroix is far from deceased.'

'In a sense,' I had to agree.

'In a sense?' she echoed querulously.

'What else can I say?'

'Dear God,' Alice said. 'How do you persuade publishers to print your unimaginative manuscripts? You seem to be lacking the one faculty which is supposed to set writers apart from the rest of us. How do you get away with it?'

'My secret,' I said.

'It's all this gritty realism. I suppose. All this seedy sex. No room for wholesome fancy at all.'

'That has to be the non sequitur of the year,' I argued.

Alice was indifferent. 'As for that book, make sure she gets it,' she said.

'Just one thing,' I said. 'In the interest of gritty realism, how does Rose manage in that house? I gather you see her regularly.'

'Weekly. As for others, there is a cleaning woman once a fortnight. A neighbour who shops for her. And a bank manager who calls in connection with things financial. That is all. Unless Pierre is tallied too.'

'Of course.'

'I have proposed a gardener. But she says she prefers to leave the garden to Pierre. It seems that he gets a poet's pleasure from flowering plants.'

'The weeds around the house don't strike me as lyrical. Doesn't she ever look out the window?'

'Not to my knowledge. No.'

'So she sees what she wishes to see.'

'She doesn't just see it. She inhabits it.'

'Inhabits what?'

'As fine a picture as she ever painted,' Alice said.

Next day I played my walk-on role in this story. I inscribed a book to a man who would never read it. The words were warm in sentiment, perhaps rather too florid. *To a fellow fantasist*, I wrote. In a furtive way, it was meant as a tribute to Rose.

Without need of a guide this time, I left Alice at home and took the route across the city to Rose Lacroix's house. With the book under my arm, I fought through hedge, weed and wild rose and arrived on her front verandah. The door was open on her hall. There was silence and shadow within. It seemed altogether lifeless. It *was* lifeless. Banging on her door, and ringing a bell for good measure, I was more and more aware of having landed myself in a ludicrous charade.

'Rose?' I called tentatively. 'Rose?'

Silence.

'Rose?'

More silence. And more.

I gave it a last try. 'Rose?'

This time there was a response of sorts. It came in a small and wandering voice. 'Darling?' she asked. 'My darling? Are you back?'

At the same time — though I may have imagined it — I found myself smelling a stale Turkish cigarette. Had there been some earlier male visitor that day? Or did a wisp of my adventure with Pierre's tobacco linger in the room? That was as much as I could surmise. Apprehension already had the better of me; suddenly my nerve went altogether. I placed the book prominently on a hall table, turned, and left swiftly. It was shameful of course — fleeing and possibly frightening a confused old woman — but I was selfishly surviving a panic attack of my own.

My first-hand experience of Rose Lacroix almost ends there. Four days later a letter arrived at Alice's home. It had been addressed and mailed by Rose's cleaning woman. Within was a note from Rose thanking me for the book I had sent Pierre. She went on to say, 'We are enjoying your stories very much. In fact we are fighting over them. Pierre says you have the touch of a true storyteller. I am less competent to judge, of course, but for what it is worth I also think your stories most interesting. May you write many more. Pierre, by the way, expresses the same wish.'

I may have read further. It is also possible that I didn't. But Alice did.

'You appear to have won yourself a couple of new fans,' she observed maliciously. 'One of them rather wraith-like, but never mind. Beggars can't be choosers.'

'Do shut up,' I said.

'Only if you fix me a gin and tonic. The story is yours if you can settle on a sunny ending.'

'Sunny?' I said.

'Don't tell me it's beyond you,' she said.

That episode was most of thirty years ago. It ended, or should have, with Alice's death, not far short of her century, three or four years later. Much of my life left with her. It was said that I looked every inch a grieving widower at the graveside. Anyway I was the only male present resembling a spouse.

With her departure there was no reason to recall Rose and Pierre Lacroix; and I didn't, or not often. My memories of Alice cloud the margins of her long existence. Rose and Pierre were of the margin.

That is, until a day last year. It began with an early morning telephone call. Any call that morning, anything short of a film contract dripping with dollars, was bound to be unwelcome. With my left hand I was getting away proofs of a new book to my publisher; with my right I was preparing a talk for English teachers on the new non-fictional mode of the historical novel; there were a dozen letters needing reply. While still trying to get up a head of steam — or, in this instance, trying to raise smoke from my second-best pipe — the telephone rang. A shaky-voiced woman asked for me by name.

'Speaking,' I said irritably.

'I am calling in connection with Rose Lacroix,' she said.

'Rose who?' I asked. For a moment I failed to comprehend.

'Lacroix,' she repeated. 'Rose Lacroix.'

'Rose?' I said with disbelief.

My imagination leapt ahead. Was I talking to an art scholar preparing a monograph on forgotten New Zealand painters? What other cause for the call?

'She is, I'm afraid, very ill.'

'She is *what*?'

'Ill,' my informant said.

'She has to be dead,' I argued.

'Not quite. Not yet.'

A large breath gave me time to tally Rose's years. She must have been something like five short of her hundred. That wasn't extraordinary. Alice, after all, had lasted as long. Then again, Alice had been living a full life. Rose hadn't. But who was I to say? I lived with phantoms too. More than just fictional, many had been cherished companions until I unwillingly mailed away the manuscripts in which they resided.

'Who am I talking to?' I asked.

'A neighbour,' the voice explained. 'I've been keeping an eye on Rose for some time. That is, since the police were called to break into the house. She hadn't been seen for weeks. They found her unconscious on the floor. She was all but dead of neglect and malnutrition. She refused to spend more than a week in hospital. She said her husband wouldn't manage without her. As I'm sure you know, her husband hasn't been sighted for many years.'

'Yes,' I said. 'I know.'

'She has had another collapse; she was taken off to hospital last night. This time it appears to be a stroke. I felt you should know.'

'What about friends and relatives?'

'Dead or disappeared. She appears to have driven most of them away over the years. Especially those who had difficulty in indulging her fancy.'

'Dear God,' I said.

'It is sad,' she agreed.

'What do you want me to do?'

'Visit her, perhaps,' she said. 'She talks of you.'

'Of me? '

'Frequently. Of what a dear friend of her husband's you have been. Of hers too.'

'Me?'

'She once showed me one of your books signed for her husband.'

'Yes, but,' I began; and ended silent.

'I'm sorry if this is a shock,' she said.

'It is,' I assured her.

'It was just the way things happen,' the woman explained. 'Driving home from the hospital last night, I happened to hear you talking on the car radio. I missed much of it, so I'm not altogether sure of what you were saying.'

'Nor was I,' I confessed. 'It may have been about the human need for stories. How nations need them. How people do. How we are constantly telling ourselves stories about what and who we are. Otherwise, it seems, we cease to exist.'

'I found it interesting, such as I heard. I took it as a signal. I should have contacted you earlier.'

'Never mind,' I said. 'You have now.'

Other chores suddenly trivial, I accompanied Rose's good-hearted neighbour to Auckland hospital. Rose was installed in a curtained-off cubicle of a geriatric ward. Most of her fellow patients also appeared to be stroke victims. Her eyes were open; she was gazing sightless at the ceiling. There was no response when her neighbour spoke. Then a gentle young doctor drew us aside.

'I am afraid I can't give you good news,' he said.

'I thought not,' the neighbour said.

'Nevertheless there is no harm in your trying to communicate,' he said. 'There *are* miracles in my line of business. People do sometimes fight their way back to something resembling consciousness. That is, if they have the will to fight. Many manage to limp along for years, though not, I think, Mrs Lacroix.'

He left us alone with Rose. The neighbour said, 'Perhaps you should try talking to her.'

I was less than happy about this.

'Please,' the neighbour said. 'Her memory may only need the one jolt.'

One jolt? For what? Rose lived as long as she could manage, with Pierre and without; there had to be an end to her vigil. Yet I took her hand and squeezed it. 'Rose?' I asked. 'Can you hear me?'

She may have been waiting on a male voice. Anyway something

seemed to stir.

'I'm Alice's great-nephew,' I said. 'Pierre's New Zealand friend. Remember me?'

She heard something, though her lips took time to find it. 'Pierre?' she said all but imperceptibly. 'Pierre? You?'

This was not how things should go. From that point I began to improvise; I had no choice.

'I'm here,' I said. And, 'I'm waiting for you.'

Her lips moved again. I took it she was asking where we were to meet.

'You know where,' I insisted. 'At our old table in the Cafe Lavena, off San Marco.'

How else to put it? Her expression was sweet.

Though we remained at her side for another hour, there was no further flash of understanding. We didn't try to force one either. She died the next day.

The funeral was modest. I was there, of course, as Alice would have wanted. Aside from the undertaker, his junior and an Anglican clergyman, there were just five at her graveside. Two — her bank manager and a lawyer from Alice's old firm — were there from professional concern. That left Rose's good samaritan neighbour and her husband; and me. There were no Lightfoots in attendance. Possibly the family had decided to write off this remote and embarrassing relative who had passed under the outlandish name Lacroix for fifty years. As things were, there were just enough male hands to carry her coffin. I found it unnaturally heavy. I didn't ask my fellow pallbearers whether they found it the same. No one else appeared to notice anything exceptional. No one else staggered as I did, briefly, under its weight. I appeared to be alone with my feeling that the coffin had more than one occupant.

Her grave had been dug, next to those of her parents, in a tree-greened corner of Auckland's rolling Waikumete cemetery. There were Lightfoots interred left and right, their headstones becoming less ostentatious as the 19th century receded and 20th advanced. Otherwise there was little there to intrigue a social historian or hobbyist genealogist. Nor would the marble marking Rose's grave, or so I imagined.

With rites ended, the coffin lowered, I was disinclined to linger for empty handshakes. I hurried away through long grass and weathered headstones. Then I heard feet behind me. It was the lawyer. 'Just a word,' he asked.

'By all means,' I said reluctantly.

'I understand you were familiar with Rose Lacroix.'

'One meeting. Many years ago.'

'Enough to form an opinion of the woman?'

'An imperfect opinion, possibly.'

'The fact is that next to no one here today — her neighbour excepted — knew her much at all.'

'Does it matter now?'

'In the matter of her will, it might. Your estimable great-aunt drew it up for Mrs Lacroix many years ago. And filed it through her old firm.'

'Alice? Did she draft it poorly?'

'It is most precise. No one in the firm has ever found cause to quarrel with your relative's paperwork. Indeed she remains rather a legend in our office. She must have been a remarkable woman.'

'She was,' I agreed. I felt a spasm of old sorrow. Thirty years hadn't cured me of Alice.

'And an unusual one,' the fellow went on. 'Perhaps not as unusual as the late Mrs Lacroix, but certainly a woman of an uncommon kind.'

'Eccentric may be the word you are looking for,' I suggested.

'Perhaps,' he agreed.

'It seems, however, you are trying to tell me something more.'

'In connection with the will. Yes.'

'You have a difficulty?'

'Let me put it this way. It presents us with a problem. There is, for example, the request that her headstone should display her husband's name beside hers. As you doubtless know, her husband is not interred here; it is by no means certain that he is dead. He could still be very much alive, in Canada perhaps, or elsewhere.'

'Anciently, at best.'

'All the same,' he said, 'the cemetery authorities might have something to say about such a deception.'

'Need they know? A work-hungry stonemason isn't going to ask questions of a customer.'

'I might well be at professional risk were I a party to the enterprise.'

'Then turn a blind eye. A little extra lettering isn't going to hurt anyone. I shall take responsibility.'

'That is generous of you. But it doesn't stop there. There is the nature of the memorial. She wished something rather out of the ordinary.'

'As Rose herself was,' I suggested.

'In brief, she wanted a sculpture modelled in the manner of Rodin's The Kiss. You are familiar with that work?'

'I am,' I said, fighting a smile.

'Further, she compounds the problem by stating a wish to have the word forever inscribed at the foot of the sculpture.'

'Forever?'

'In especially large lettering. One could take it as a proclamation of sorts.'

'Indeed one could,' I said, my smile now altogether out of control. 'Is there a law against it? A civic regulation?'

'That is the odd thing. It appears not. There seems to be no precedent at all. But it is bound to cause controversy. Stone angels are acceptable in this location. Lovers, as we know, are not angels. Especially not Monsieur Rodin's.'

'In a year or two no one except Sunday strollers in the cemetery would give it a thought.'

'Perhaps,' he agreed. 'But The Kiss is extremely carnal.'

'By its nature,' I allowed.

'Then you agree?'

'Agree?'

'That her request might be overlooked?'

'On the contrary, I think her notion rather splendid.'

'Be it on your head, then,' he sighed. 'By the way, should you be wondering, her estate is to fund an annual poetry prize in the name of Pierre and Rose Lacroix.'

'A poetry prize?'

'In their joint name. An extraordinarily generous one, if I may say so. It seems to surprise you.'

'Not as much as it might,' I said.

'That brings me to one final matter. It concerns you personally. You are named executor of her paintings. This should not be too onerous. She appears to have had no standing in the art world. I am given to understand that her paintings are without value. The frames, on the other hand, are useful. They may fetch a respectable price from a dealer in fashionable junk.'

'In which case, I am happy to spare her paintings the same fate.'

'Good God,' the lawyer said. 'There must be a hundred. What will you do with them?'

'Use them for a sunny ending,' I decided.

'This late in the day? Besides, sunny isn't a word I should choose, especially not in present circumstances.'

'It isn't my choice,' I said. 'As you have no doubt heard, my great-aunt frequently expressed herself in unconventional fashion.'

'I see,' the fellow said, but didn't and couldn't. 'I rather regret that I didn't know her.'

'Sometimes I rather regret that I did,' I explained.

The paintings of Rose Lacroix (at my insistence, under the name Rose Lightfoot again) went on public show for the first time a month ago. The exhibition was prefaced by a good deal of publicity, engendered largely by the memorial risen on a northern slope of Waikumete Cemetery. In the end Auckland's disconcerted civic fathers and cemetery authorities, made to appear puritan and petty, put up no fight. It helped, of course, that Rose came from a once prestigious pioneer family. (After decades of neglect New Zealand's founding fathers are now in fashion, forgiven their ruthless ways, their relics and diaries now flushed out from cobwebbed attics.) For reasons unclear to me Rose's eminent ancestors seemed to exonerate Rodin's twosome of steamy misconduct in a public place.

Controversy meant that her exhibition drew people by the hundred rather than the dozen. Perhaps two or three thousand Aucklanders trooped through the exhibition by its end; on weekends there was even a modest crush. Many of the visitors were elderly, near contemporaries of Rose, leading grandchildren or great-children along; others were in wheelchairs. These longtime residents of the Auckland region gazed with wonder and sometimes sorrow at the isthmus city Rose once celebrated, now lost to developers, demolition gangs, and designers of charmless glass towers and chintzy shopping arcades. Critics wondered at her tidy, eerily tranquil vistas and vied with each other to affix labels on her oeuvre: regional romantic, colonial realist, provincial naturalist, naive nationalist. Yes, and primitive too. Primitive? Rose had forgotten more about art than these professional windbags ever knew. Anyway no label was adequate; all missed the mark. Rose Lightfoot remained singular, outside genre, beyond both tributary and mainstream, a one-woman movement without a wisp of contemporary concerns. It was agreed only that there had been no more meticulous a chronicler of early 20th century Auckland and its environs. *Forgotten Forerunner Found*, trumpeted the heading above one review. The glow in her work had less to do with paint than with innocence, simplicities gone. **Study the world attentively**, said the manifesto on her wall, **so that it can be expressed truthfully**. And who would dare say she was never art's handmaiden? My notes for the exhibition catalogue, listing the few significant events in her life, left much to the imagination. The gaps were filled by a powerfully ideological essay, by a female critic of some reputation, which pictured Pierre Lacroix in sinister shades and Rose in saintly radiance. She now promises to become a feminist martyr of the front-line kind.

It should be recorded that the paintings sold. The one dissonant note was that the proceeds went to finance a literary prize — a prize, moreover, as much in Pierre's name as hers. My feeling, of course, was that it should have been to reward painters wrongfully unsung, not poets publicly congratulating themselves on their linguistic wizardry. But Rose had all she wished: the memorial, the inscription, that prize in their name. Pierre Lacroix could never escape his Venetian bride now. Though he would never know it, at least in this life, he was paired with Rose Lightfoot for not a day less than forever.

PART THREE

The Birds of Grief Gully

GREAT-AUNT ALICE hovered witch-like above me in my infancy. She may have been minus a broomstick and black cat, but such lacks were no handicap when she had a high-powered spell to cast. I was in terror of her tongue from the time I was three years old. (I may have left a more benign impression of Alice elsewhere, but that, as the familiar phrase goes, is another story.) As a mid-term juvenile I was even more aware that she was not an adult to be taken lightly. In her presence I was even cautious about breathing. I kept a distance and, if that feeble strategy failed, my mouth stoically filled, desirably with ice cream and cake. I could also loiter interminably in the toilet until sure peril was past. Later teenage tactics, such as burying my head sulkily in a book, didn't thwart her. She would snatch the book from my hand, hold it at arm's length, and snort. Her most disparaging sounds were reserved for novels by such as Rider Haggard (he of *She*) and Edgar Rice Burroughs, the man who enriched literature with tree-swinging Tarzan and his hairy apes.

'If you persist in reading rubbish, ' she warned, 'you might even finish up writing it.'

That, she implied, was the worst of fates. Did she know something I didn't? Alice was always ahead of the play. No one could say I wasn't warned.

'Can I have it back now?' I pleaded, meaning my book.

'In due course,' she said, and added, 'At your age I had that indolent habit too.'

'What habit?' I asked.

'Letting authors tell me what a book is about. Don't let them push you around. Consider following my practice. When an obviously unworthy book comes my way I don't necessarily heave it across the room, no matter how tempted. I read the first page, then the last page, and fancy the rest — that is, everything between.'

Demonstrating this procedure she ripped the heart from the nearest book to hand. She then presented me with the first and last pages; the rest, to my consternation, went to a wastebasket.

'There,' she said with a flourish. 'You are now free. Your imagination can roam unhindered.'

I tried to divert her before she disembowelled more of my library. 'How do the stories turn out?' I asked.

'With some inconsistencies and a few loose ends,' she admitted. 'Not that it matters. The currently fashionable view, I gather, is that the story isn't everything; that it only gets in the way.'

A storyless book wasn't my notion of a good read, but I allowed her to continue baffling me to the best of her ability.

'There is more to a book,' she added, 'than print on a page.'

'More?' I asked wearily. 'Like what?'

'The habits of homo sapiens. A most mystifying species.'

'In what way?'

'We can't get enough of ourselves. What happens when we are bored silly by our own lives? We entertain ourselves by diving into the lives of others — in books, films, or plays — and not coming up for air more than we must. Make sense of that, if you can.'

I couldn't begin to. For the record I have just taken a deep breath. I hear Alice's sigh in my ear as I set this down. She was explaining herself.

Alice was becalmed in the last decade of her life before I found her easy company. By then in my thirties, I had begun to give her as good as I got. Scores were now surprisingly even. Her heresies were subject to overnight revision if I was inconsiderate enough to agree with her. It wasn't perversity on her side, or charity on mine. She may have been on her last legs; she wasn't going to finish without a fight.

It was about then that she weighed up the world and tallied her years and decided that there might be some point to me after all. For one thing I was more available than most of her friends and relatives. Though she had large reservations about the life I led and the books I published, she saw that I might function as an archivist, stockpiling such of her past as she would admit to.

'Get it right,' she warned. 'Which means nothing fancy.'

Little embellishment was needed. Alice was extravagant enough. Her past was long, lively and seldom commonplace. Early in the field as a female lawyer, she had also once stood for Parliament. (Unsuccessfully. Even seasoned feminists considered her excessive.) During the depression of the 1930s she brazenly risked arrest by blocking tenant evictions, marching with the jobless and homeless and ducking police batons. She was also denounced as a sinister rabble-rouser for raising money to bandage bleeding victims of Spain's civil war. But her past went back further, to the turn of the century and before. Alice was born in 1877, in the spring of colonial New Zealand and the summer of Queen Victoria's reign. I sometimes fancied that her footwear was still coloured by the dust of pioneer roads. In the resonant intervals between her narratives (on the occasions she drew breath) I imagined hearing axes biting into giant trees, men blowing hills apart to win a route for roads and railways, horses whinnying, wagons clattering and the fragrant drip of rain through unfelled forest. I had been absent in Europe too long, attempting to make a writer of myself; I had returned as a writer, but a stranger in the land. Alice made it her business to ensure that I didn't persist in limbo.

Our conversations were as amiable as Alice allowed. There were skirmishes and sometimes pitched battles, especially over the high ground.

'There is one thing I can't help noticing,' I said.

'Notice away, then,' Alice commanded.

'Your memories are peopled rather densely with hermits.'

'Hermits?' she said.

'Runaways,' I prompted. 'Outcasts.'

'Really?' she said, shamming surprise.

'Really,' I said.

'Why not say lovers?'

'Lovers?'

'The best hermits are. They are far less forgettable than most who flutter through the stories of someone I refrain from naming.'

'So I've been writing about the wrong people?'

'You said it. Not me.'

'Those you recall are a middling lot too,' I pointed out.

'In one way, if not in another,' she allowed.

'Meaning what?'

'If you can't see why they make themselves memorable, it's time for an eye test. Your novels might literally improve out of sight.'

'Why should they intrigue you?'

'They seldom fail to leave questions behind. Little mysteries.'

'And that's it?' I asked. 'That's all?'

'For the most part. For more of my childhood than I care to remember there seemed more recluses around than citizens of gregarious character. Perhaps an empty land made friendless wayfarers conspicuous. There was hardly a secluded riverbank without its resident hermit boiling a billy. And not many miles of road without a bearded man on the swag looking for somewhere to rusticate for the rest of his days. Pioneer left-overs. Frontier relics. Victorian residue.'

'There's more to it,' I suggested.

'Envy,' she said.

'You mean you fancied the notion?'

'I rather think I might have made a very fine fist of it.'

'I can't see you lasting long in hibernation.'

'You not only need an eye test,' she observed tersely. 'You need a hearing aid too.'

'Anyway,' I went on, 'I don't see that hermits have much to offer. 'What if we all sequestered ourselves? Where would we be then?'

'Happier,' she asserted.

'Come on,' I said.

'As a lawyer I was, thank God, never briefed to appear on behalf of the human race,' Alice said. 'I should have been obliged to inform my fellow defendants that it was in their interest to enter a guilty plea to everything in sight.'

That was in character. Alice's suspicion of her fellow human beings hadn't diminished with the years. Even the depression didn't leave her on a leftward tack for long.

'As for solitaries,' she continued, 'they come out of it clean. They don't organise wars. They don't hound the poor for being poor, the old and feeble for being old and feeble. When the last trump sounds, and the last charge is read, they at least are likely to have an acceptable alibi.'

'Because they weren't around?'

'In short,' Alice agreed.

'I fail to see absence from the scene as a prerequisite of virtue.'

'Then you hardly know the half of it.'

'Don't tell me,' I said. 'You are now going to acquaint me with the rest.'

'If you are seen and not heard, and eat all your greens,' Alice promised.

Alice grew to womanhood on New Zealand's northernmost goldfields in the last years of sail, the last decades of horse and buggy, and the first of movies, motor vehicles, and machine guns: most of her early life was on and around the arresting limb of New Zealand called the Coromandel Peninsula. There were — or had been — gold mines north and south, large and small, in every cranny and canyon; for much of its length the peninsula was perforated with man-made caves, tunnels and deeply dug shafts. Her father was a mining engineer involved, among other things, with the famed Martha Mine, destined to become the richest repository of bullion in the British Empire. More than a century on, and five monarchs later, men with tractors and excavators are still trawling for the Martha's yellow treasure. The rackety, shuddering mining towns and townships of Alice's era — with thunderous stamper batteries pounding quartz reef to rubble and finally to docile ore — have mostly gone. A windowless cottage here, a vandalised schoolhouse there. Stumps of concrete where batteries and mine-heads once stood. Few other relics remain. There is no more than a tiny and tactfully worded plaque recording the infamous labour struggle fought here with pistols and clubs and ended with the killing of a strike leader. Sheep and cattle graze the emerald hillsides where men burrowed.

Alice seldom recalled her childhood as other than enthralling. Her parents were a cheerful and frankly amorous couple, as bawdy as colonial convention allowed. Her brothers and sisters, of whom there were many, were exuberant in character too. Tears seldom lasted long in the household; laughter outlived sobs. As for their environment, the mining towns may have been ugly and noisy, but solitude of a sylvan sort was seldom more than a short walk away. So were swift streams, cool pools, and waterfalls lavishly framed with fern. Family walks were frequent. Her father was a tweedy, pipe-smoking rambler in the hearty Victorian manner; he believed it built character as well as good health. As they trooped along forest trails they chanted the Latin names of trees and plants as one. (Attention to the classics was considered character building too.) The sea was no long journey either, especially not on horseback. The hills and bays of the peninsula remained bright in her memory for life. From the age of sixteen, especially within her family, she was judged a talented watercolourist. Her paintings, particularly of New Zealand's indigenous flowering plants, were remarkable for their botanical precision. It would have surprised few had she journeyed off professionally in the direction of science or art. The problem was that she could not take her gift seriously, nor flowering plants. 'Botany is boring,' she pronounced. 'All flowers think about is sex.'

Alice was no dilettante in that realm herself. It was on the Coromandel goldfields that she first kissed a boy — in fact, several — and finally eloped with the schoolteacher who became her first husband. They fetched up in Auckland and married there when parental consent was reluctantly given. Conjugal happiness was brief. Her handsome young husband died a year or two after they exchanged vows, but not before fathering twin daughters. Though her family rallied around, and forgave her all, Alice was unnervingly long in retreat. Her toddler daughters, Lucy and Jane, finally tugged her back into the world.

Decades later she began camping out on the Coromandel, in childhood's seductive domain, first with her children, later with her grandchildren, often with all. Perhaps ghosts were being laid. Who knows? Alice was the last person to ask. These nostalgic excursions became annual. On one such she met up with Jim and Laurel Bird. Alice was under the impression that there was nothing left in the world to surprise her. Jim and Laurel were to dispel that illusion.

According to Alice, Jim Bird made his first appearance on the peninsula in 1903. The year matters less than the decade. The old Queen was dead; a philandering prince was enthroned. Jim Bird meandered out of that interim era. He was an unassuming sort of fellow, lean, sandy-haired, good-looking, and young, maybe with something on his mind. Thoughtful was how most described him. In company his eyes often wandered elsewhere. It was a long time before people learned where. On his maiden visit to the peninsula he merely wandered into town, like many footloose and jobless men of that time, and moved on after a week or two. What distinguished him from others on the swag was that he didn't seem in urgent pursuit of employment. He had no problem with money; he could afford a respectable room in the Star and Garter. He could also pay for his own drinks in the bar and occasionally for those whose conversation interested him. Above all, he had the air of a man who knew what he was up to, leaving others to guess. People may have remembered him because he didn't add up. His clothes may have been dusty, his possessions modest, but he was tolerably well spoken, possibly with an education behind him. If he was a man with a patchy past, as some surmised, he was in no haste to confirm it. Few would have been surprised if that past had included trouble with the law, though there was no evidence for this. Others claimed to know more than they really did of the fellow. One ex-townsman asserted that he had seen Jim working as a teller in an Auckland bank. Another seemed to recall him as a talented rugby winger — or was it champion sculler? — from somewhere up north. This may have been so. He could have been a hundred other half-remembered men. (Not that anyone asked.) His seasoned face also suggested he was someone lately familiar with the world's wilder climes. No one tried to verify this either. His cool eyes didn't invite questions. Nor was he free with his real name. When obliged to give one out, he styled himself Dave Smith. The casual Christian name suited him; the near anonymous surname was less felicitous. It was to be a long time before he was known rightly as Jim Bird.

There was another puzzle. Though plainly a man of sensitivity, there was leather in his handshake; he was not a fellow unfamiliar with living rough, or with hard labour. He had the wiry physique typical of men at home in a shearing shed. So what was he, then? A remittance man? Some black sheep of a titled family summarily dispatched to the colonies for bleaching? Without anything said, this supposition was dismissed too. It failed to accord with his sober character. Remittance men, for the most part, were bad drunks. Though he was fond of his whisky, Jim's intake was moderate.

Finally rumour fitted him out as a professional geologist furtively on the hunt for minerals, perhaps silver or copper or new veins of peninsula gold. It did not seem too wide of the mark. Nothing else explained his lone hikes into the mountains, his residence in abandoned mine tunnels. If he discovered anything of consequence on these excursions, he wasn't saying.

Still travelling light, he left as quietly as he came. But he was back again the following summer. On this second visit he was riding a horse and leading a packhorse. He spent less time yarning with locals in the bar of the Star and Garter and more in the ranges behind the town. Men watched him disappear upland, looked at each other, and shrugged.

The slender Coromandel Peninsula was heaved from the Pacific floor, in a fit of planetary pique, millions of years before man put in an appearance. Proofs of its disorderly origin are many. Bulky ramparts of volcanic rock rear above ferny rain forest and luminous beaches. In the South Pacific the Coromandel's stark silhouettes are rivalled only by those of Tahiti. There is little level land: it is mostly valley and peak, height and hollow. Humans found its fretted coast hospitable; its rocky coves and sandy bays were settled perhaps a thousand years ago. In the early 19th century, however, it was depopulated by musket-bearing Maori of a northern tribe. Musket and massacre, followed by fatal contagion, heralded Europe's arrival. At first the overdressed newcomers wished timber, especially that of the kauri, for naval masts and spars; it had become, from the time it was first worked, the world's most coveted marine wood. The whale of the vegetable world, the kauri is second only to California's sequoia in antiquity and height, and in terms of cubic feet the most impressive timber tree in creation. (Its obese trunk can be mistaken for a silvery cliff-face.) In up to 2000 years of life it can climb two hundred feet high from the forest floor. Like the whale, the kauri soon seemed due for extinction. It was a kauri-hunting British vessel — H.M.S. *Coromandel* in 1820 — which gave the peninsula its exotic name. Before long teams of axe-swinging, saw-pushing tribesmen were emptying the peninsula of its wealth. Logs surfed down waterways, sometimes splintering wastefully over waterfalls, on their journey to seafarers with order books to fill. Demand — from as far away as Sydney and San Francisco — always exceeded supply. For decade after decade, the length of the peninsula, the great trees toppled. They made their last stand, beyond the reach of axe and saw, on inaccessible ridges and summits. Elsewhere the forest was left scrappy. Fire often followed the sawyers.

Before that enriching rush finished another began. Gold was glimpsed in a peninsula creek as early as 1852. At first there was insufficient to be persuasive. Moreover it was not easy to win. Little of it was alluvial. Most was embedded in quartz. Lack of alluvial colour meant it was not a poor man's field. Lashings of capital and purgative doses of cyanide were needed to make such a goldfield relinquish its largesse. The colonial government was loath to pay out a promised reward for the meagre discovery. And since Maoris were at that time unfriendly the find was not investigated further. It was not until the late 1860s, after Anglo-Maori battles had passed the peninsula by, that a second strike was made. It was timely. Northern New Zealand, and particularly the untidy town of Auckland, was mired in depression. Between one month and the next the peninsula was seething with disillusioned soldiers, impoverished farmers, optimistic clerks and bankrupt shopkeepers. There were even clergymen in search of their bedazzled parishioners.

So much for the 19th century. By the beginning of the 20th, when Jim Bird showed his face for the first time, the peninsula was passably serene again. Gold was now in short supply. So was worthwhile timber. The population had halved. Fishermen and farmers had become more commonplace than sawyers and miners. There were still a few ageing prospectors foraging in the hills. Jim Bird, it seems, made their acquaintance as he excursioned in the ranges. Professing an innocent interest in the time-hallowed tricks of the gold-seeker's trade, he shared their evening fires and listened to their yarns. Still posing as an enthusiastic amateur, he even learned how to make and work a one-man quartz crusher ingeniously regulated by a bent sapling which permitted an iron-capped pole to crash down on a stump and pulverize quartz placed there. By summer's end, when he disappeared again, he had won enough gold to justify his Coromandel sojourn. His grizzled companions were left to imagine that they had seen the last of him. They had not.

He was back again for a third summer. No longer a novelty, the fellow passing as Dave Smith was soon just another seasonal face, due a friendly nod and no more. That, though no one was to know it, was his wish. Anonymity was his need; he wanted to be overlooked. There was a flurry of fresh interest in the fellow when it became known that he had taken up some land in the hills. Not just some diminutive miner's claim, but a respectable parcel of acres. Though livestock wasn't evident yet, he had enough land to graze a cow or two and a modest mob of sheep.

'In Grief Gully,' one townsman reported.

'What would he want that for?' another asked.

The answer was a shrug. Jim Bird, alias Dave Smith, was judged to have a screw loose. Grief Gully was more valley than gully. Otherwise it was all its name said. Some steep miles back in the ranges, it wasn't an unattractive locality. It sloped lumpily to the sea and looked north to the sun. There were silverings of Pacific beyond leaf and fern. The problem with the place was that it promised much and delivered little. Likely leads in the quartz — leads which elsewhere might have heralded a useful lode — mysteriously shrank into insignificance. Sometimes these leads almost literally wisped away with the first stroke of a pick. If this was God's handiwork, one frustrated fossicker said, it was enough to make any bloody Bible-banger a blaspheming atheist overnight. Perhaps due to some last subterranean spasm, as the peninsula cooled, the rock structure was eccentric. Bash away at it as men might, blast and burrow as they did, one sure result was debris. There was never a lack of rubble in Grief Gully. Nor of blasphemy. But it made a base for a novice prospector not noticeably in need of a fortune. Jim had no pride in the matter of working patiently through leftovers.

'All right,' Alice said. 'So what do we have so far?'

'God knows,' I said.

'I am not especially interested in what the Almighty might make of it,' she said. 'I'm interested in what you do. What happens now?'

There was a silence.

'Pass,' I said.

'Come on.'

'He must have been up to something,' I suggested.

'He must indeed,' Alice said.

'Or running from something.'

'That too,' Alice said.

'Both?'

'Both.'

I tried to get my head around this. I couldn't.

'Consider the date of his first appearance,' Alice suggested.

'1903?'

'Exactly. Look at what was going on in the world, or had been. Look at a young man wandering the country. Where might he have been?'

I tried. Then it came. I asked, 'Hadn't the South African war just ended? The Boer war?'

'Sometimes you aren't as dense as you seem,' Alice decided. 'What more do you know?'

'That it was fairly squalid. No one, especially not the six thousand

New Zealanders involved, thought it was a war to be proud of. Some seemed to feel that there was more to be said for their determined adversaries than for their blundering British commanders. As I recall, the New Zealanders even called a strike against their officers.'

'Nine out of ten,' Alice said.

'Why not ten?'

'You persist in ending sentences with a preposition,' she explained.

Ex-journalist Jim Bird and his amiable mate Luke Perham were working out a tree-clearing contract north of Auckland when the war began. It wasn't their first such contract. They had been a respected team, roaming from one North Island region to another, taking what work they could, for most of five years, or since Jim found an outdoor life more rewarding than filling rural newspapers with columns of parish pump news. Among fellow farmhands, labourers and foresters he now had a modest reputation for bush ballads of his own composition. Clipped from magazines where they sometimes found print, his anthems to mateship, and the camaraderie of the open-air life, were often to be seen pasted on the walls of shearers' quarters and lonely musterers' huts. The seasonal inhabitants of such huts, normally unsentimental men with work-hardened hands, were also known to carry his ballads in pockets close to their hearts. Though academics might mock the notion, and scorn the creaky character of his diction, it might be surmised that something in Jim's bittersweet ditties gave meaning to the lives of such men. (The other sex didn't get much of a hearing in his rhymed lines, but that was nothing new.) The *Auckland Weekly* sometimes featured his work; likewise the celebrated red page of the *Sydney Bulletin*. There he shone in the reflected light of such eloquent bards as Australia's Banjo Patterson (*The Man from Snowy River*) and New Zealand's Thomas Bracken (*Not Understood*). Luke, though he would never say so, was proud of having so singular a mate at his side. It was not unknown for Luke to suggest the subject of Jim's next literary venture. He was always first to read something fresh from his mate's pen. And he loyally took umbrage, sometimes with fists raised, when insensitive associates, perhaps frightened of something soft in themselves, found it necessary to belittle Jim Bird and his ballads. Life in New Zealand's backblocks wasn't altogether as comradely, nor as lyrical, as his verse suggested.

Their fast-riding boss brought word of hostilities on a spring day in 1899. Insubordinate Boers of southern Africa had begun making themselves a nuisance to the British Empire by denying civil rights to English speakers resident in the Transvaal; their unashamed aim was to drive Britons out altogether. They followed this with an impudent ultimatum for the withdrawal of British troops. With the ultimatum past, war was no longer talk. New Zealand was mustering a force to help subdue these avowed enemies of the empire — a force which, so politicians claimed, would prove the country's devotion to Britain and win favours from the motherland in the future. Britain's most loyal colony had volunteered its contingent — with unhappy haste, some thought — two weeks ahead of the war. Even the *Iliad* does not record fighting men speeding to the fray a fortnight before formal brawling began: Agamemnon, Ajax and Achilles seemed dawdlers.

'I daresay you'll be itching for a crack at the buggers too,' the boss observed. 'I would if I was younger. Any young buck would.'

Luke looked inquiringly at Jim.

'Don't think about it,' Jim advised.

'Why not?'

'You're almost a married man.'

This was true. Luke was due to wed a sweet-natured girl named Laurel Green in a month or two, or when their current contract was worked out. Luke lately talked of little else. Laurel was the daughter of one of the few affluent farmers in the district. Unlike most of his neighbours, her father had been on the scene early, buying up the best-looking hill country, and leaving less promising land to latecomers; his healthy flock was widely envied. So was Luke, after his headlong courtship of Laurel. He was judged in on a win. Laurel was the best marital bet for miles around. Not only was Luke about to marry into a prosperous family; he was also about to acquire an especially lovely and lively-eyed wife. A schoolteacher loved and missed by her pupils, Laurel had returned to the family home to care for her father on the death of her mother. Quiet, bookish, and a stylish dresser, Laurel remained something of a city girl. Unlike her loose-living brothers, she was attentive to her father's needs. Luke had no problem winning paternal approval for the union. With unreliable sons, Mr Green was happy to welcome a sturdy son-in-law to the farm. What he couldn't have counted on, however, was Luke's conviction that rural chores lacked something in adventure. That, roughly speaking, was the position now.

'What about you?' he asked Jim. 'This war interest you?'

'I'm not in a rush to think on it yet.' Jim said.

'You mean you might go?'

Jim knocked ash from his pipe. 'If I get round to thinking about it,' he explained with irritation.

'There'd be yarns to tell,' Luke said slyly. 'Maybe a few new ballads in your swag.'

'Maybe,' Jim allowed with reluctance.

'You'd get to see the world too,' Luke pointed out. 'The way I see it, it isn't damn fair.'

'What's not?'

'You free to see a war and not me. Why should you have all the fun?'

'Because I haven't met a girl as good as Laurel,' Jim argued. This had truth. Though still in his twenties, Jim was already resigned to a bachelor existence. Unlike Luke, he had never been a ladies' man. He still found females fairly much of a mystery. War might give him more to think about than failure with women. A Boer bullet tickling his scalp was bound to banish introspection. And if the worst came to the worst, who would notice him missing? Luke maybe, for a year or two. Next to no others. His parents were dead; he had lost touch with remaining kin. That made him a model candidate for war.

At this point the boss intervened. 'I'll tell you what,' he said. 'If either of you go, or both, we'll call quits on the contract. I'll pay you out for what you done, and a bonus beside. How's that?'

'Better than fair,' Luke said. 'You can pay me out for a start.'

'Luke,' Jim pleaded.

'It's my business,' Luke said defiantly.

'It's also Laurel's. Speak to her first.'

'She'll understand. She'll have a man worth marrying.'

'Heroes don't make good husbands,' Jim argued. 'They're inclined to finish up dead.'

'Why look on the black side?'

'Because there is one,' Jim said.

'The way it sounds,' Luke said, 'it could be all over in weeks. If we aren't quick we could even miss out. There'll be others kicking down doors to join up.'

'Maybe,' Jim said. 'It doesn't mean you're obliged to. Or, for that matter, me.'

'If I don't go I mightn't forgive myself,' Luke claimed.

'If you do go, Laurel mightn't forgive me,' Jim pointed out.

'Why?'

'For one thing she'd blame me for not talking you out of it. For another, if you broke a toe she'd hold me responsible.'

'Why should it matter to you?'

'Because it would,' Jim said. More than that he couldn't say. He remained sorry he hadn't set his cap at Laurel himself. Unlike the lusty males of his ballads, Jim was seldom single of purpose: there were fewer pitfalls in pen and paper than in trying to win a woman. Indecision, not for the first time, had been Jim's undoing. While he dithered, Luke swooped. Laurel might have said yes to Jim's invitation to a country dance. She might even have been interested in hearing him read his manly verse. Then again, she mightn't. Laurel was a girl of educated taste and Jim wasn't Shakespeare. Yet she might have responded with warmth had he made himself plain. The way things were, he was never going to know.

'You still thinking on it?' Luke asked.

'On a reason for going,' Jim reported. 'Perhaps I just found one.'

'Like what?'

'Like keeping you alive for Laurel,' Jim said.

Luke thought it a laughing matter.

Luke last saw his fiancee at a railway station, among scores of equally tearful womenfolk. A large Union Jack floated overhead, with a hundred smaller versions fluttering in juvenile hands. A brass band was thumping out patriot tunes. Hoarse dignitaries, having waded through their loyal speeches, were calling for three British cheers. Jim did his best not to look at either moist-eyed Laurel or restive Luke, though Laurel once met his eye. She appeared to be telling him something, or trying to, but last minute uproar and the locomotive's steamy whistle made it impossible to hear. Finally, through gusts of vapour and billowing streamers, she blew him a despairingly fierce kiss. As the train shunted away with its cargo of apprentice warriors, Jim wondered what he should make of that phantom kiss. Weeks later he was still wondering. She might merely have been reminding Jim of his promise to look after Luke. On the other hand she might have been signalling something else altogether. Either way there was now no way of Jim knowing. What mattered was that her eyes had been shiny with something unsaid.

The volunteers camped outside Wellington until a ship was ready to whisk them to Africa. Their training was modest and hasty and largely involved horses. This, unlike interminable parade ground manoeuvres, made sense: they were soon to meet a mounted enemy and the war might be determined as much by the calibre of horses as by the character of men. They learned to jump horses over fallen logs and treacherous ditches, to familiarise skittish beasts with the sound of gunfire. Target practice was conducted behind the cover of prone mounts. Not that all this was demanding to men of New Zealand's first contingent. There was hardly a volunteer without talent as horseman or marksman or both. That included Luke and Jim.

Punishing last minute drill curbed high spirits. On the whole, however, they couldn't have been away to war much sooner. They took their own horses. In those unsophisticated times young men actually paid for the privilege of warring for the empire; they were expected to provide their own equipment, even to fodder their beasts on the long voyage to Africa. Serving their sovereign was a selfless and sometimes prohibitive enterprise, costing close to sixty pounds a man, or one or two thousand dollars in today's currency;

some went into debt for the privilege of pursuing Boers across South Africa's desolate veldt. Their allowance from Britain's coffers, when it trickled through, barely amounted to beer money. On the other hand levelling incomprehensible Boer farmers wasn't the same as lowering New Zealand trees; it wasn't meant to be enriching. Their reward, so they were frequently reminded, was in proving their worth, in serving the Queen with distinction. Courage, not cash, was the point of the enterprise. Their deeds, or so their superiors informed them, and jingoist song-writers attested, would reside imperishably in history's golden pages. The justice of their cause wasn't worth discussion. In failing to respect Britain's flag, South Africa's Boers were cold-hearted monsters. Queen Victoria herself was leading the charge. 'A horrid people, cruel and overbearing,' she judged. Primed by such as their sovereign, half the population of Wellington turned out to cheer the colony's valiant young away. They were to be the first colonials to arrive on the battlefield, heading off the Australians and Canadians by hundreds of nautical miles.

As promised, adventure was waiting. So too, given new rapid-fire weaponry, was carnage of an efficient sort. That was not altogether as expected. Nevertheless New Zealand's rough riders — casual and swaggering, with their dusty horses, slouch hats, bandoliers and carbines — made themselves look sufficiently fearless for photographers.

Critics weren't lacking when they presented themselves for inspection on arrival in Cape Colony. 'There is a want of ingrained discipline in these men,' one British general was heard lamenting. The Boers, however, took a longer view. They saw men much as themselves, possibly more to be respected than indifferently fed and led British regulars and their bewhiskered and sluggish superiors. The New Zealanders were soon familiar with shots warning them off — first at Naauwpoort in the course of an otherwise unexciting reconnaissance, and then at Arundel, where they collided carelessly with a Boer position and were fortunate to escape with only horses slain. Jasfontein was the site of their third misfortune; it was where their first comrade fell. The Boer sharpshooter who brought him down was unlucky not to topple more.

Otherwise boredom was nine-tenths of the war. Much of the remaining tenth was the battle to keep it at bay. Irritable officers ameliorated monotony by keeping their charges up to scratch with disciplinary details and field punishments. The least lovable officers were not high-pitched lieutenants and opinionated captains fresh from Britain's halls of martial learning. The worst were New Zealanders masquerading as Britons, aping their imperial overseers and braying superciliously at their fellow colonials.

The flashest of this breed was a bulky and bullet-headed officer named Timms. Captain George Timms provided his fellow New Zealanders with someone to curse before Boer snipers began picking them off. Always slow with salutes, New Zealanders were even more lax in Timms' vicinity. British officers were overbearing enough. Counterfeit Britons always had to go one better, to double up on detentions. Timms would possibly have enjoyed proving his mettle by presiding over a court martial and pronouncing a death sentence. Fortunately for many, and especially for mutinous Luke, a firing squad never came Timms' way. He had to make do with spread-eagling delinquents painfully on a wagon wheel, a form of punishment justly called the crucifixion.

There was more to the man. The New Zealand press was in need of heroes. The more heroes, the more headlines. The more headlines, the more volunteers. After the Naąuwpoort skirmish, survival under fire at Arundel, and the near catastrophe of Jasfontein, the New Zealand contingent had to be possessed of a hero. And so it soon was. To the bafflement of those under his command, that hero turned out to be Captain George Timms. No matter that he had been seen hysterical when Boer bullets first fell among them at Naauwpoort, and had been saved from disgrace by a level-headed lieutenant ordering men to stand their ground. At Arundel Timms had been seen crouched sweatily in the lee of a kopje — a rocky hillock — while urging men forward. Fortunately it was an indifferent day for rebel sharpshooters; no New Zealander fell. Timms' incompetence more or less matched his cowardice. At Jasfontein, after misreading a map and overruling junior officers, he had stumbled into occupation of a vacated Boer farmhouse and its outbuildings. This, so even lowly corporals saw, had the makings of a trap. Timms had barely established his men when Boer rifles began banging out; the landscape was instantly alive with three score enemy and New Zealand's first casualty was expiring on the battlefield. Timms, seeing no painless escape from encirclement, ordered his force to return fire. The siege, as inconsequential as any in a lightweight war, bobbed back and forward for some hours. Huddled behind barn walls, the New Zealanders found the near sounds of shot, shattering windows and splintering rock more acceptable than the screams and whimpers of a dying comrade. He lay a score of yards from the farmhouse and not much more from the nearest Boer.

Though never a chum of this trooper, Luke was quick to his feet. 'Who's going with me?' he challenged. 'Who'll bring him in?'

It seemed Luke was all for winning a Victoria Cross before his first month's soldiering was out. On the other hand there was no doubting his sincerity. He didn't like animals suffering either. Though reared in a colony which thrived on the supply of eviscerated beasts to Britain, he had always preferred taking woodland apart.

Seconds later Jim was also on his feet. Then a third man stood. Unfortunately for Luke's prospects as a bemedalled hero, he had made himself too audible. Captain Timms was in hearing. His head low, and frequently flinching, he crawled along the line. 'What in damnation is going on here?' he called.

'We're going to fetch Trooper Bradford back,' Luke explained sunnily.

'Have you heard an order to that effect?'

'Not to any effect,' Luke admitted.

'You are hearing one now,' Timms informed him. 'Return to your place in the line.'

'Sir,' Luke pleaded.

'No ifs and buts,' Timms insisted. 'I need every rifle busy. Furthermore I'll have you on charge for refusing an order in the face of the enemy. That, as you may not live to learn, is a serious matter.'

'So is what's happening to Trooper Bradford,' Luke pointed out.

Jim saved Luke from prolonged martial unpleasantness. A prudent corporal, as he now was, he dragged Luke to earth and, with a sharp elbow in his side, encouraged him to keep the peace.

Moving off cautiously on his belly, Timms could be heard asking a lieutenant, 'What's the name of that wretch?'

'Perham, I believe, sir,' the officer replied.

'I'll remember it,' Timms mused. 'Insubordination is like a weed in a garden. It is better dealt with before it becomes rampant.'

'Indeed, sir,' the discreet lieutenant said.

Five minutes later, unable to stand the sound of the dying man themselves, two Boers chanced British bullets and compassionately dragged him to a trench where he could succumb to his wounds in more comfort. Captain Timms was not heard from further. Luke made his satisfaction plain. He also made an enemy.

New Zealand's first full day under Boer fire was ended by the arrival of a party of British regulars, undersized men who soldiered with no visible grievance and retrieved casualties only when ordered. Their shooting was impressively dour too. When they had pushed the Boer besiegers out, fantasy moved in. An unedifying tussle became a blistering victory under the African sun. The New Zealand press had been waiting impatiently for a worthwhile battle and decided that this had the ingredients to please armchair belligerents. 'Though the Boers endeavoured to breach their line again and again,' reported a fervent correspondent, 'the dogged New Zealanders proved impossible to dislodge from their rocky perch. In their first real baptism of fire our slouch-hatted daredevils gave the Boer a day to rue.'

This was news to the rough riders. It seemed they alone noticed that they had been party to a needless fight and fortunate to escape graves alongside Trooper Bradford's; they seemed surrounded by liars and lunatics. They marvelled even more when they learned that Captain Timms was deemed the day's hero. It seemed the first New Zealand trooper to fall was not a sufficiently inspiring nominee. So it had to be Timms. (The Britons who actually lifted the siege went unmentioned.) 'Indifferent to his own safety, Captain Timms marshalled his men again and again for courageous thrusts at the enemy,' announced the same imaginative correspondent. Anxious to acknowledge the arrival of their colonial cousins, British commanders weighed in with praise and promotion. Overnight Captain Timms became Major Timms, with a moustache waxed in the manner of British officers. This makeshift man of the hour became the first colonial to command a unit on behalf of the British Empire. It would be months before an Australian or Canadian was so honoured. The qualms felt by Timms' former peers, especially concerning his fidgety conduct under fire, went for nothing. It was done. He walked off with the first Distinguished Service Order awarded in the war; his demeanour encouraged the belief that he was setting his sights still higher. Luke and Jim and fellow troopers found themselves even more under Timms' thumb. For a time Timms did his best to live up to his reputation; who would not, with the applause of the empire ringing around? Anyway he was to be in evidence at the relief of Kimberley and other engagements as rich in headlines. Growing celebrity tended to keep Timms out of the way of his men — something both tactful and compassionate, since he continued to inform them they were spineless curs, cowards and morons. He left menial details to lieutenants. He was fêted here, interviewed there, and photographed shaking hands with generals. Newspapers arriving in from New Zealand made it plain that he was now a national hero. Taking a dim view of this, Jim, Luke and most of their comrades were even more overcast when they learned of Timms' past from a law clerk turned trooper. It appeared that George Timms' peacetime record didn't warrant close inspection. He had a reputation for personal violence, and had been lucky to escape conviction more than once. A slippery lawyer and hobbyist soldier before he heard the call to arms, Timms had also headed off financial scandal, and probable arrest and trial, by leaping into uniform ahead of most in the colony. There were tales of an even murkier nature, some involving beardless youths. At least for Timms, it was a well-timed war.

'We should have bloody known,' Luke said.

Jim's first man-to-man exchange with Timms was no more auspicious than Luke's. In charge of a latrine detail, and leading by example,

Jim was labouring sweatily under noon sun. Then Major Timms, making one of his infrequent personal appearances, came into view. Since circumstances weren't conducive to pretending himself blind, Jim mustered a salute. In return he received the frigid stare for which Timms was famed.

'Corporal Bird, is it not?' Timms asked.

'That is correct, sir,' Jim agreed.

'Is it right, then?'

For a moment Jim was mystified. Was Timms inviting him to express a view on the wisdom of the war? 'I'm not sure what you mean by right, sir,' he said.

'Mess talk tells me you have a high opinion of yourself as a literary fellow.'

'I wouldn't say that, sir.'

'No? So what would you say, Bird?'

'That I have no opinion of myself as a literary fellow, sir. On the other hand it's true that I write verse on occasion and sometimes see it in print.'

'I'm not interested in modesty, corporal. I like a straight answer. Is it not the fact of the matter that your name is known?'

'That might be said, sir,' Jim agreed with caution.

Erstwhile lawyer Timms, keeping his hand in, plainly felt a waspish interrogation served circumstances best.

'Might it also be the case,' Timms went on, 'that you are looking for something to write about here? That you might already be writing it?'

'I don't take your meaning, sir.'

'Then let me be blunt, Bird. Rumour tells me that some seditious doggerel has been circulating in the New Zealand contingent. Its most objectionable feature, so I am informed, is that it encourages disrespect for superiors. Someone has to be responsible for the vile stuff. You, it seems to me, have the necessary credentials. Have you anything to say to that?'

'Not particularly, sir.'

'Why not? Disappointing you, is it? This war?'

'I didn't say that, sir.'

‘Be damned careful you don’t,’ Timms warned. ‘Should I learn of anything further likely to undermine morale, I won’t have to look far for a culprit. I have a reputation as a man who means business. Are we understood?’

‘We are, sir,’ Jim said.

In camp that night, Jim handed pencils, pens and notebooks to his mate. ‘What’s this all about?’ Luke asked.

‘Temptation, ‘ Jim said. ‘Lead me not into it.’

Even in peace some men soak up evil much as salt sucks moisture from the atmosphere; in war’s noxious climate even more is abroad. To magnify his reputation as a man meaning business Timms had a recalcitrant Boer scout brought before him for questioning. The fellow was unwilling to talk, though Timms pressed a pistol to the back of his neck. Even to those disposed to believe the worst of their superior, the shot came as a surprise.

Graves were soon dug with more proficiency. Otherwise martial undertakings remained mystifying; British commanders left onlookers with the impression that they were still fighting the battle of Waterloo, this time unluckily. The Boers went to ground, exposing themselves seldom, proving even more hazardous in rocky bastions. They sallied out only to make life miserable for Britons. This was effortless. The soldier’s dread of a visible enemy gave way to the terror of an invisible one. Familiar with the unfriendly terrain, the Boers used it to powerful effect; they could be anywhere and everywhere and often were. Mounted troopers riding peacefully on patrol might, a moment later, be in breathless battle for their lives. There was menace in every outcrop of rock, in every clump of growth.

In late 1900, weeks after the best Boer units had been scattered, months after the war might have been won, Timms’ team of rough riders, along with a column of Britons, was assigned to consolidate Britain’s authority on ground lately wrested from the enemy. This amounted to torching Boer dwellings and townships, penning bitter captives behind barbed wire, and pillaging their stockpiles of foodstuffs, much of it on the hoof. The New Zealanders commandeered steers and sheep and bayoneted turkey and geese. The rough riders were not in the habit of going hungry. On the other hand even full stomachs did not persuade them of virtue in their role. Some crept off in the dark with nourishment for their prisoners; guards looked the other way.

'A weird old war,' Luke complained. 'If we wanted to fight farmers, we could have stayed home and scared some silly.'

Despite their best efforts, home was even more remote. Now incomprehensibly considered an expert on the reading of difficult ground, Major Timms came riding in after surveillance of the area with a British general named Mahon. Scouts, among them Luke and Jim, had sighted a weary Boer column making camp between two scrappy lines of kopjes. The treeless ground to the left was crowned by an abandoned enemy laager. The kopje to the right was scrappily wooded, battle having passed it by. Bluff General Mahon, with a couple of calamities behind him, cautiously determined on harassing the departing rebels from the rear at first light. To do so in dusk might involve him in more misfortune. Artillery would train punishing fire on the Boer encampment and the surrounding ground. Then a flying column would hit them. The evidence suggested that the enemy was in no condition to give fight. 'Tomorrow promises to be lively,' Timms informed his men.

Luke took a more pessimistic view. 'I got a funny feeling we've been here before,' he whispered to Jim.

It was not like Luke to be apprehensive. He had a reputation not only for drollery in dismal circumstances but also as the fighting cock of the New Zealand contingent. He had several times scrambled off solo and returned with bewildered Boer prisoners. 'No more than a day's mustering back home,' he claimed. No New Zealander was having a luckier war. To Major Timms' irritation, some of Trooper Perham's feats, having caught the ear of a scribe, had found their way into print. This meant less flag-waving prose devoted to Major Timms. To no one's surprise, Trooper Perham's detentions became longer.

'How do you mean we've been here before?' Jim asked.

'With Timms before he got famous,' Luke explained. 'It's only a matter of time before the bugger drops us in the dung again. By my reckoning the time's about now.'

Jim recalled Jasfontein with unease. 'Who knows?' he said.

'*I* know,' Luke said.

Luke's gloom persisted in their canvas-covered bivouac that night. Outside, a warm wind plucked at tent ropes, and horses grazed hungrily. Luke remained cheerless. Perhaps the strain of proving himself a worthwhile soldier had caught up with him. His silences were eloquent. Finally it seemed that he wanted to talk of Laurel.

'If I'm not mistaken,' he said to Jim, 'you got some feeling for Laurel yourself.'

Jim didn't find reply easy.

'Did I say that?' he asked.

'Maybe not. But you look it. I got eyes too.'

'So what are you trying to tell me? That I'd steal a mate's girl?'

'I'm just telling you that whatever you feel about Laurel is all right by me,' Luke said. 'If I'm cashing in my chips I'll feel better knowing you're around to look after Laurel.'

'This is ridiculous,' Jim said.

'I've had a clock ticking in my head for weeks,' Luke said. 'This afternoon, when we crawled uphill to look on that Boer column, the ticking stopped. Just like that. Stopped dead. What does that mean?'

'A powerful imagination,' Jim suggested.

'Don't you ever take me seriously?' Luke said.

'Not if I can help it, Luke. No.'

'I'll tell you what it says to me. It says there's a bullet headed my way.'

'Come on,' Jim said. 'Who doesn't have nerves?'

'It isn't nerves talking, Jim. It's me.'

That said, Luke seemed more composed than fearful. It didn't improve matters. Jim would have preferred persisting melancholy.

'I don't need to hear any more,' he decided.

'You're going to,' Luke announced. He fumbled in a tunic pocket and found a crumpled photograph, a portrait of Laurel. The photographer was a competent one. A connoisseur of womanhood, he had missed little of Laurel's warmth and nothing of her shapely character.

'Do what you like with the rest of my things,' Luke said. 'This picture's another matter, though. It's special. See it's buried with me. And tell her too.'

'Luke,' Jim said in despair.

'Take it,' Luke said with ferocity.

Humouring Luke, Jim tucked the photograph in his own tunic pocket.

For once morning went as planned. Shells dropped among the Boer encampment. Then Mahon's flying column fell upon them. Soon a white flag rose. A dozen Boer wagons and several ambulances with wounded were captured and a hundred prisoners taken. Britons then directed artillery fire on what was seen to be the last of the Boer column, retiring at speed. Few shots were received in return, fewer worth ducking. This action, though of no great worth, would possibly salvage General Mahon's reputation. Meanwhile Major Timms was busy brushing up his own. He ordered a lieutenant to prepare a patrol of thirty reliable men. Jim and Luke found themselves in this party.

'We shall scout the kopjes to the right,' Timms explained. 'A British column will be passing through tomorrow. We are to ensure they suffer no inconvenience from loitering snipers. Every kopje must be seen cleansed. Our column is to provide a clear path. Are we understood?'

No one said not.

'And, by the by,' Timms added, 'I shall be keeping you company.'

There was relief on several faces, most distinctly on Jim's. Luke's forebodings might soon be seen as unjustified. A patrol involving Timms was sure to be circumspect. Indeed some suspected that their commander was spiriting up a chore to keep his name conspicuous in dispatches. At the least it would be mentioned in conjunction with General Mahon's.

Jim edged his horse into line beside Luke's. Luke barely acknowledged his presence; he was looking stiffly ahead. The thirty horsemen then began advancing in open order, with an interval of ten yards between files. Thorny vegetation lifted to their left, tall heaps of rock to their right.

'Corporal?' Jim heard. He looked around and saw Timms.

'It cannot have escaped your attention, Bird, that we're without our customary companion on the right flank.'

'No, sir. We're all sorry about Sergeant Ryan.'

'Take his place today and his third stripe is yours.'

'Thank you, sir,' Jim said with no perceptible gratitude.

'No more than that to say?'

'Only that I can't help noticing that the hills ahead weren't hit by shells this morning. Someone seems to have missed General Mahon's orders. The gunners took a holiday.'

'You wouldn't be trying to tell me my job, corporal?'

'I'm telling you what I see, sir.'

'Indeed, corporal. And as you should also have seen, the Boer is in retreat, all spirit gone.'

'We must hope so, sir.'

'Good,' Timms said. 'Just one further thing concerning your promotion. I am obliged to point out that your continuing association with that insolent wretch Perham does you no credit.'

'I can't help that, sir. He's an old mate. We joined together.'

'Am I meant to be impressed?' Timms asked.

'I'm just explaining, sir. And while I'm at it, I have a favour to ask.'

'Of what nature, man?'

'It concerns Trooper Perham, sir. He's not in good shape.'

'I have had no report of a wound.'

'His trouble is more of a mental nature, sir.'

'Mental?' Timms' laugh was short. 'Mental?'

'Mental exhaustion, sir.'

'If you're telling me the bugger's mad, that's no news.'

'Nevertheless,' Jim pleaded, 'I'd be grateful if he were excused duty and allowed to drop back.'

'Where do you think you are, Bird?'

'I'd like to think I was among men of decency and compassion, sir.'

Timms failed to take this personally. 'Your request is refused,

Bird. We should all be the poorer if Trooper Perham were deprived of his usual heroics. Mental trouble? What next?'

'Sir,' Jim began, but found nothing to say.

'Carry on corporal,' Timms ordered.

A small, dustily overgrown kopje had begun rearing before men on the right flank. Jim's instinct said to skirt it. That, however, was not Timms' notion. It was to be seen safe.

'And no flinching,' Timms told Jim. 'Set an example. Convey my orders as crisply as you can. Remain in earshot and in touch.' He dropped back three files to enliven others of his party.

Horses began labouring uphill, some led by men warily afoot. But for the frothy breathing of their beasts the day was quieter still. Jim again nudged his horse protectively beside Luke's. He was powerfully tempted to urge his mate to his rear. Should he do so, however, others might panic; there could be an undistinguished flight. Then again, that was more desirable than arguing with a Boer fusillade.

'What did Timms want your ear for?' Luke said.

'He says I'll make colonel if I write something singing his praises.'

This didn't win a wisp of smile from Luke. Sunk in his saddle, his posture remained that of a man awaiting the worst. Jim, meanwhile, persuaded himself that Timms might know what he was doing. The thought proved helpful until the worst struck. It arrived in the form of explosive bullets from a Boer rearguard. At a range of fifty yards, discharged through fissures in natural battlements, their rifles were more than usually venomous. Men, where they could, rolled away from their expiring beasts. Others remained down with their horses.

Timms, to the rear, attempted an order and fetched up something felicitous from his repertoire. 'Files about, retire!' he called.

Jim couldn't believe it. Files about, retire? *Files about, retire?* The order might have produced something pretty from men and horses disposed on a parade ground. It was elegant madness with shot crackling around, men and unhinged animals adrift on crumbling ground. More fatally still, Timms' amazing order meant that Jim's lacerated right flank would now be the left, and vice versa. Men of the left flank, as the right had become, were seriously out of luck again, in place for a second bloodbath. Jim saw what was coming; he was familiar with the damage that fifty dedicated Boer rifles could do. Luke was among those on the imperilled flank, drifting even further into danger. A dozen Boers might already have him in their sights. If they hadn't, they soon would. At this point nothing but an untidy bolt from the field would save them.

Hoping to make his superior see virtue in informal departure, Jim spurred his horse toward Timms. 'No, sir,' he shouted in anguish. *'No!'*

Timms was riding in showy circles and exciting himself with a revolver.

'You're off your flank, corporal,' he announced. 'Nor have you given men my order.'

'It's impossible, sir,' Jim protested.

'Impossible?'

'Your order, sir. A sharpish retreat out of Boer range might save my flank. Your order won't.'

'Give it,' Timms said.

'Sir,' Jim pleaded.

'Give it,' Timms hissed, using his revolver for emphasis. 'Make it work.'

Jim would never be able to plead that he had misheard his commanding officer. He dropped back to gather up scattered men. For much of the war he had been wondering how much fear he could manage, or how little; he was now due to learn.

His message was slow coming, his mouth too dry. 'Files about, retire,' he heard himself whisper and then hoarsely call.

The following confusion, with men bunching and wheeling in panic, proved useful for Boer purposes; they had a fairground shooting gallery, though their targets were often shadows in dust. Their shot began ripping into files before retirement had begun. More mounts went down; there were unhorsed troopers running blind, desperate for shelter, and others abruptly prone.

Jim looked over his shoulder to see how Luke was faring. With survivors of the thinned left flank, he was still manfully trying to make sense of the order while imposing himself on a rearing horse. In the next moment there was little of Luke to recognise. Smoke issued from his head and chest as expanding bullets burst inside him; streamers of brain, lung and blood floated briefly to his rear. His horse carried on a few yards before its rider pitched faceless from the saddle, not a word said.

Unwilling to see what he saw, though he would revisit it for the rest of his years, Jim pushed toward the thorny scrub into which Luke had tumbled. At the same time he rallied demoralised troopers. He even persuaded a few to push forward, find cover, and make use of their weapons. 'Nothing stupid,' he ordered. 'Just draw fire from me.' He slapped his own horse away and continued on foot. Rather marvellously, Boer shot began to diminish. Perhaps marksmen were taking time off from their labours to marvel at a man so bent on suicide. As others recounted it, he travelled fifty yards, passing through enemy fire upright and unsinged and managing to place rounds in the vicinity of the Boer position. He travelled the last yard or two carefully, as if spiky vegetation were his problem. Then he knelt to Luke and rolled him over. He could have fitted his fist into the hole in Luke's chest; there was also little left of the back of his head. Jim's hands came away sticky. Though Luke was still warm, all life had gone. Accepting it at last, Jim stood to empty his rifle at the Boer marksmen. Few replied. The Boer rearguard was moving out, having inflamed the British Empire enough for one morning. Then he became aware of shouts and hoofbeats to his rear. He turned his head toward the source of these sounds. It was Timms and an unhappy lieutenant. Timms reined in, unable to manage either his frisky mount or his fury. 'What in hell do you think you're up to, corporal?' he roared.

'Making your order work, sir. Not to speak of calculating the cost.'

Timms decided to ignore this. 'My impression is that you have been telling men to go to ground in contradiction of my order. True?'

A Boer parting shot skipped from nearby ground. Timms ducked needlessly.

'I could tell a lie,' Jim said. 'It wouldn't be worse than some that get told around here. And will be.'

They were eye to eye. Jim's meaning was plain.

'I'll have your guts,' Timms promised.

'You're welcome to my stripes,' Jim offered. 'As for my innards, maybe not. I might just make a point of having yours first. That's if I can find them.'

'Did you hear that, lieutenant?' Timms asked his subordinate. 'Did you hear insult and threat?'

'I did, sir,' the shaky officer agreed.

'Remember it well. You will be required to repeat it in formal circumstances. Meanwhile have the bugger put under guard.'

Jim's deliverance came in rotund and red-faced form. With the last Boer banished, General Mahon rode in. He had been witnessing events through binoculars. He was not impressed. He had, however, observed a solo corporal refusing to surrender ground and rallying his fellows to give fight.

'The man's a credit to you, Timms,' he said. 'With a hundred of him we might all start packing our bags.'

'Yes, sir,' Timms said weakly.

'Well?' Mahon said. 'Where is the fellow? Aren't I allowed to shake his hand?'

Timms' face was a picture. Jim's, though bleaker, told a story too.

Wounded were borne off in ambulances, and the dead wound in blankets for burial. Jim made a point of digging Luke's grave. Ceremony was brief, with Timms reading approved gospel verses. Men bent their bare heads, slouch hats held over their hearts, as five rifles cracked skyward. There was a departure from custom at the end. Jim stepped forward, with something in the shape of a letter; he seemed intent on delivering it to the grave.

Timms, ever vigilant, scented an irregularity. 'Stop,' he ordered. 'What's all this?'

The burial party relaxed, leaning on shovels.

'Well?' Timms asked.

'Just a photograph, sir,' Jim explained.

'A photograph? By now you should know photographs are useful in enemy hands. They use them for their boastful propaganda. They are also helpful for their intelligence officers. Photographs, like personal effects, can tell them which of our units are about.'

'Not this one,' Jim claimed. 'It couldn't be more innocent, sir.'

'I am the best judge of that, corporal.'

Jim protested, 'Trooper Perham gave it to me, sir, in the event of his meeting up with a bullet. He wished it interred with him. I promised I'd see to it.'

'Then let me inform you that you and Trooper Perham are gravely out of order, altogether in breach of standard practice.'

'Trooper Perham is no longer with us, sir,' Jim pointed out.

'That is no sufficient excuse,' Timms determined. 'Regulations state unequivocally that all personal effects shall be surrendered to officers and returned to relatives. No exceptions are noted.'

Was this true? It didn't matter anyway. On the stony veldt Timms composed his own code of conduct. Present circumstances didn't provide for Jim paying a lawyer to argue the point.

'The photograph is of the woman he was to marry, sir,' Jim pleaded.

Timms was unmoved. 'Pass it over, man. I shall take charge of it. As for Trooper Perham's mental problem, that may be considered cured.'

In pain, Jim surrendered the offending item. For the second time that day he had difficulty forgiving himself; it sickened him to see the photograph wrenched free of its wrapping and considered at length in Timms' beefy fists.

'A lively looking wench,' he judged. 'Yes, by God. Perham didn't deserve this bit of skirt. What's your impression, corporal? Eh?'

His sweaty face loomed uncomfortably close to Jim's.

'My impression is that you're a miserable bastard,' Jim said with some warmth.

First from the left, then from the right, Timms' fists crashed into his face. Minutes later Jim was back under guard, spitting blood, with a lone thread dangling where his stripes had been.

'We were supposed to be talking about your runaways,' I reminded Alice.

'Were we?' she said. She enjoyed being vague. She also had a good line in senility.

'You know we were.'

'Perhaps.'

'What do you mean perhaps?'

'You'll see. Some stories go wandering off by themselves. They don't like being shut in. They need to breathe the air around. That reminds me. You've been doing some rambling yourself.'

'What does that mean?'

'You were in late last night.'

'Me?' I said innocently.

'Remarkably late for a man professing himself finished with women under the age of ninety. When am I going to meet her?'

'That might be a little premature.'

'What's wrong? Do you think I'd frighten her off?'

'If you must know.'

'It seems rather premature for you to be staying out late. Your former marital bed is hardly cold.'

'My former marital bed,' I pointed out, 'disappeared in the legal division of spoils. The hours I keep, if I may say so, are my affair.'

'Also mine if you assault my sideboard at three in the morning.'

I attempted to change the subject. 'Talking of noise, is there more war ahead?'

'Minus Boers,' she said inscrutably.

Jim Bird's war ended with enteric fever rather than a court martial. Sickness sank more rough riders than lethal Boer commandos had sniped. Though his flesh melted away with frightening speed, he was left with enough to stay in business. After long delirium, during which he was heard ordering persons unknown to ride hell for leather, Jim Bird was delivered to a ship bound for New Zealand; doctors judged him better out of war's way.

He was not the only one pronounced unfit to carry on. Major Timms, with no illness or injury, was found wanting too. In his case it was as a leader of men. Embittered accounts of his behaviour travelled home with discharged veterans. Overreaching himself, he had also begun telling politicians their business, refusing to return invalids to New Zealand when ordered. This couldn't be countenanced, even from a certified hero. On the other hand Major Timms' reputation still had uses. A compromise was found. A last burst of publicity, with stress on his military feats, camouflaged the nature of his recall to New Zealand. After the cheers and speeches, after the patriotic public placed an engraved gold sword in his hand, he was further rewarded with a decade of undiluted obscurity. No one saw where Timms went after the ceremony finished. Given his ill-concealed fondness for liquor, it was probably in the direction of the nearest bottle. The sword was later sighted in a pawnbroker's window.

Jim's return was less conspicuous. With other ailing troopers — and minus one or two dozen companions consigned to the Indian Ocean — he was landed emaciated on an Auckland dockside. There was no band, no streamers, no speeches. Nor were photographers in evidence. The wounded and wasted arrivals were a poor advertisement for proceedings in South Africa. Strident desk officers, strutting about in polished riding boots, ensured that the men were borne fast to hospital.

Reckoned surplus to requirements by the army, eventually determined robust again in hospital, Jim took a train to see where it stopped. Then he purchased a horse to see where it led. If Luke's wish was on his mind, he didn't make it apparent; he didn't point himself north towards Laurel. For a time he weaved about with small concern for the points of the compass. Then circular motion stopped. Looking around, he found train and horse had carried him south. Jim had never been one to argue with the fall of the cards. He needed to find himself more likeable before he attempted to chum up with the world again; he wanted time to think things through. Workmates seldom found him comfortable company; his moody silences unnerved them. His ballads of the Boer war, the ones Luke looked forward to reading, remained unwritten.

For a year he sheared sheep, harvested flax, threshed grain, drained swamp and fenced grazing land for farmers in need of labour. Was he trying to slip Luke's shade? If he wasn't in one way, he was in another. He worked his way south until he ran out of land and looked out on sea. That night, in a creaky bed in a cheap hotel, he dreamed Luke and Laurel were marrying. Laurel was resplendent in white and Luke handsome in a dark suit. Next morning, finding himself peaceful, Jim Bird pointed his horse north. On the strength of nothing in general and everything in particular, he reckoned himself fit to look up Laurel. Remorse had shrunk to regret.

Towns large and small fell behind. Sheep country drifted by, cattle country, and patches of old forest too. Past Auckland he was in familiar territory. The scrubby hills he and Luke cleared were now shiny with grass. Five miles short of his goal, he bedded in a pub he once patronised with Luke. The publican was new and not conspicuously amiable.

'You look like you been travelling,' he observed.

'I reckon,' Jim agreed.

'Far?'

'You wouldn't believe it.'

That was true. No one would.

'You'd be looking for a job, then?'

'Or maybe a wife,' Jim confessed.

'You'd be lucky,' the publican said.

'Why would that be?'

'There's no women going spare in this neck of the woods.'

'No?' Jim said.

'Good-lookers don't last long around here,' the publican explained. 'Daughters head for the city. They take one look at their mothers. They see them old before their time. Hard country makes hard faces. So off the girls go.'

Jim thought to skirt the subject. 'There was a family called Green around here.'

'Still is,' the publican said. 'Out along Ten Mile Road.'

'Know much of them?'

'Not much more than the name on their gate. They don't bring their custom here. They keep to themselves.'

'There was a girl. Laurel.'

'Was there? Come to think, maybe there was. The one who lost a fellow in the war?'

'That's the one,' Jim said eagerly. 'Heard anything of her?'

The publican meditated. 'Maybe,' he said, 'but nothing I recall easy.'

'Try,' Jim suggested.

'As I recollect, there's been changes up that way.'

'Changes?'

'For starters, old man Green isn't up to much any more. He took a bad fall from his horse last year and walks with a stick. His sons buggered off to Auckland, after a family fight. The old man's been hanging on.'

'But the girl — Laurel — she's still around?'

'I haven't heard different.'

'You said there's been changes.'

'There's talk since the new man arrived,' the publican admitted.

'New man?'

'The one managing the farm for old man Green. I can't say I know much about him. Nor does anyone else. Binns, I think his name is. He seems to have got his foot in the door. That's if I hear right.'

'If you hear right about what?'

'The Green girl,' the publican explained. 'The one you was asking after.'

Jim was silent.

'You up to another drink?' the publican asked.

Jim was.

Next morning he saddled his horse and pushed it along Ten Mile Road. It was a spring day, growing warmer, with a pleasing whisper of breeze. Hills flecked with sheep travelled by. For a time he found himself reading ridges, rocks and vegetation with suspicion; he could still fancy a fusillade in his vicinity.

Late in the morning he sighted the outlying acres of the Green farm, soon the high Green homestead too. On the rising road ahead, in the middle distance, there was a man leading a horse and a dog yapping at a reluctant mob of sheep. This lone and bulky figure was still too far off to yield a face; anyway the fellow had his back to Jim. Yet there was something familiar, something to which Jim couldn't put a name. He rode on until almost abreast of the preoccupied musterer. Then he called a country greeting. By this time fewer than thirty yards separated the two men.

The fellow looked up with a start, his face filling with surprise. Jim also found astonishment difficult to mask. The publican almost had the name of the fellow right. It wasn't Binns. It was Timms. The former Major George Timms. He looked at Jim as though a salute was still in order. He didn't get so much as a cool ghost of a greeting. Meanwhile his horse closed with Jim's.

'Corporal Bird?' he said, his expression rather sickly, as if he'd been caught with his hand in the till.

'Bird does me now,' Jim said. 'Plain Jim Bird.'

'What in damnation are you doing here?'

'I could ask the same of you,' Jim suggested.

'I am what you see,' Timms said. 'We all have to put that tiresome war behind us. No doubt you've done it your way. This is mine. So what do you want?'

'I'm thinking to present my respects to Laurel,' Jim explained. 'I also have an apology to make.'

'That's rather unnecessary,' Timms argued. 'The past is past.'

'I'd like to hear that from her.'

Timms was even less friendly.

'It could be a long wait,' he said. 'I won't stand to one side while you stir her up.'

'Tell me one thing, then. You married to Laurel?'

'Not at this point.'

'But you got hopes.'

'Who wouldn't? She's an attractive girl.'

'Tell me if I got it wrong. She's still a free woman, then?'

'In the legal sense, perhaps.'

'So there's nothing to say I can't say hello. No regulations to say so. Have I got that right?'

Timms was silent.

'Make it short and sweet,' he said finally.

'It might be short,' Jim said. 'I can't guarantee sweet.'

'Ride on up to the homestead,' Timms said. 'I'll be along when I've got this lot pastured. Mind you don't give her a fright. She's a nervous girl.'

'Laurel? Nervous? That's not how I remember her.'

'She'll get over it,' Timms predicted. 'Women never know their minds.'

'And not many men,' Jim suggested.

'Speak for yourself,' Timms said.

Laurel was at the rear of the homestead, weeding her way through a flower bed crowded with bloom. There was no way of making a discreet appearance. For one thing, a chained dog began barking. Laurel looked up. Colour left her face.

'Jim,' she said shakily, almost inaudibly.

'That's the name,' he agreed.

She rose with a rush. He was in her embrace.

'Where've you been?' she asked.

'If I said everywhere, it wouldn't be far out.'

'But why so long? You could have written.'

'Some things are better said,' he explained.

'About Luke?'

'Mostly.'

'They've been said,' she disclosed.

'By Major Timms?'

'Mr Timms. He prefers that now.'

'I reckon he would.'

She missed Jim's meaning. 'He told us all we needed,' she explained. 'He even gave us the photograph Luke carried through the war. He said it was Luke's dying wish that he return the photograph personally to me and make my acquaintance.'

'Which he did.'

'Indeed,' she said. 'He went to much personal inconvenience to return that photograph and to assure me that Luke died a painless death.' She paused, perhaps with lingering doubt. 'Luke did, didn't he?'

'He didn't hang around,' Jim confirmed.

She led Jim into the cool living room of the homestead. Windows framed large rural views and tidal streams meandering through mangrove forest. 'I still can't believe you're here,' she confessed.

Jim had difficulty crediting it too. But he saw why things were as they were. He recalled picking up a tea-stained newspaper in a musterers' hut, dated not long before Timms found it desirable to vanish. Through the blurred print Jim learned that Major Timms had made a last attempt to win back public favour by visiting bereaved families, wives and sweethearts whose sons, husbands and suitors had served under him in South Africa. The article left the impression that he was a politician running for office; perhaps Timms did have Parliament in mind. But by that time there were more legitimate heroes in favour with the New Zealand public. Rumour, insisting on Timm's unsavoury side, had done its worst. A journalist and photographer had been on hand to record these awkwardly contrived encounters. Timms had evidently struck a vein of sympathy at the Green homestead. The photograph he saved from an African grave had proved a winning card.

'He doesn't look much inconvenienced at the moment,' Jim observed. 'I have the impression he's very much at home.'

'My father, the way things are, can't do without him.'

'Can you?'

'Can I what?'

'Do without him.'

'No one can say he isn't helpful.'

'That wasn't what I asked,' Jim pointed out.

'It is all I can say.'

'Are you happy, then?'

'Not particularly. Not since Luke died. But that is to be expected.'

Scrubbed and decently clothed after his morning muster, Timms was suddenly at the door. Then he was all but filling the room.

'Is it whisky, then?' he asked Jim. He grabbed a bottle from a shelf and banged it on the table. Two glasses also appeared swiftly.

'Too early in the day for me,' Jim protested.

'Never too early for a fighting man,' Timms asserted.

'I got nothing to prove in that respect,' Jim said.

'So I noticed,' Timms said. 'To tell the truth I never knew what you were doing in Africa.'

'You had me wondering too,' Jim said.

'Ever write more of that verse of yours?'

'The war wasn't worth it,' Jim said.

'Then we agree on something,' Timms proposed.

He filled a glass and downed the whisky neat. He wasn't slow to refill it. The second time his hand shook a little; the bottle rattled inauspiciously against glass and good liquor slopped to the floor. Looking sidelong, Jim detected apprehension in Laurel's eye; apprehension, pain, and perhaps more.

There was no mistaking how things stood. Timms may have been bruised, but he wasn't broken; he also had the makings of an ugly drinker. In such matters there was no smoke without fire. Trembling hands and tinkling glass suggested that the war still had business with Jim's one-time commander.

'You told Laurel what you wanted to tell her?' Timms asked Jim.

'I've been giving it a try,' Jim said.

'And you're happy now?'

'I'm hoping to learn whether Laurel is.'

That left a silence. Laurel was slow finding her voice. When she did, it was faint.

'I'm happy,' she said.

Jim knew about as much as he was going to know.

Timms was contemplating yet another filled glass. He said, 'Don't let us detain you if you're expected elsewhere.'

'I'll make it known,' Jim promised.

'You could eat with us,' Laurel suggested. 'And there's always a bed.'

Jim couldn't see himself under the same roof as Timms. 'Thanks all the same,' he said.

Tension ended when Laurel's father laboured into the living room on his stick. 'Jim Bird,' he said, his pleasure instant and his hand thrust out; the old man had always had a liking for Jim. 'You've been missed around here, especially at haymaking time.'

'After the war, I felt fancy free,' Jim said.

'You could have let us know where you were.'

'I wasn't sure myself,' Jim explained.

'So what now? Back to stay?'

'I'm still looking around,' Jim claimed. 'I got almost enough saved to buy a small farm. I might just do that.'

'Around here?'

'Who knows?'

He watched Laurel's face. Her expression, suiting the situation, was mixed.

'It depends,' he added.

Her reaction to that wasn't disheartening either. Had she got his message? Jim soon thought it time to leave; he found his feet slowly.

'If we can help settle you down, just say so,' Mr Green offered. 'There's always work here. Isn't that right, Mr Timms?"

Timms was far from elated by the prospect of taking on Jim as a hand.

'Thanks,' Jim said. 'I'll keep it in mind when I finish sorting myself out.'

'What does that mean?' Mr Green asked.

'Repairing my head,' Jim explained.

Timms was doing damage to his with a fourth whisky.

Taking her chance, and to Timms' evident displeasure, Laurel walked Jim to the front gate of the farm.

'You'll be back?' she asked, as he fitted his foot into a stirrup and swung into the saddle.

'Given half an excuse,' he promised.

'When, then?'

'Maybe before the year's out.'

'We're not getting any younger,' she observed.

He looked back and waved as he took the Ten Mile again. Her

wave wasn't lacking in warmth either.

For one reason and another, mostly connected with making his bank balance respectable, it was well into the new year before Jim was free to point his horse back to the Green farm again. By that time he thought himself the equal of any misfortune he was likely to meet. He hadn't written to Laurel; he imagined it likely that Timms nosed through her mail. Short of the farm, however, he tripped over news. An old shearing-gang acquaintance, propping up the bar of a roadside pub, informed him that old man Green was no longer around; he was in hospital. Worse, it seemed Jim had left his run late. Time had been on Timms' side. He had just married Laurel. Jim felt the world shift underfoot.

'Just?' he said weakly.

'Hardly a month back. You ask me, it was all for show.'

'Show?' Jim wasn't sure he understood.

'For respectability,' the acquaintance explained. 'With old Green out of the way, it didn't look right for an unmarried woman to be living with that manager on the farm. Not any more. I heard it was all rushed through.'

Jim, after buying his informative companion a drink, and a second for himself, rode on anyway.

His approach to the Green farm was more cautious this time. No dog signalled his arrival. For a time the place seemed uninhabited. Then Laurel emerged from the house with a laundry basket and began pegging out the day's washing. Among the items she was arranging were three pairs of hard-wearing men's trousers. He viewed her in silence, so long as it felt right and until it didn't. Then, tethering his horse, he called her name. This time there was no rush to embrace him. She let him come to her.

'It's true, then,' he said.

Her eyes quivered.

'I'm sorry,' she said.

'Did you think I wouldn't be back?'

'I didn't have time to think anything.'

'Was there trouble?'

'After you turned up. Yes.'

'What kind?'

'Mr Timms — George — said he'd walk off the farm if you were made welcome here again. He said you were the most deceitful and untrustworthy soldier he saw in the campaign, unfit to sit at a decent table. You know what it would mean if he walked off. I'd be running the farm alone. He laid down the law. He said he was no casual labourer. It was time things were put straight.'

'Meaning marriage?'

'Nothing less would suit him.'

'You're telling me there wasn't a choice?'

'Not with Dad in hospital and me alone.'

She shivered. There was a slow tear. 'If only you'd said something,' she said.

'My mouth was too full,' he explained.

His mouth still was.

'There was more you wanted to tell me, that last visit,' she said. 'More about Luke perhaps.'

'It doesn't matter,' he decided. 'Not any more.'

'Why not?'

'You are now Mrs Timms,' he said.

'Then it must matter, ' she argued.

He took a large breath. 'It won't make you happy,' he promised.

'Go on,' she insisted.

'There was no love lost between Luke and Major Timms,' Jim told her. 'Never.'

'True?' she said feebly.

'He wooed you with a lie. Your father too.'

After that, it was easy. Jim didn't flinch even when it came to reporting how Luke died. Nor did he omit his own spineless showing. Among other things he told Laurel the truth about the photograph Luke wished in his grave. Finally Jim disclosed his promise to Luke; his promise to look after Laurel.

'You made a poor job of that,' she said.

'And a worse one of myself,' he told her.

More might have been said. More wasn't. A voice lifted powerfully to their rear.

'Hello, then,' it said. 'What the hell is this all about? Laurel?'

Timms was upon them without warning. Matrimony seemed to suit him. His cheeks were fleshy, his body carrying more bulk. He had a rifle slung on one shoulder, a brace of blasted native pigeon on the other, and gore to his elbows.

'Well?' he said. 'Laurel?'

Getting no answer, he looked at Jim.

'If I were you, Bird,' he said, 'I'd throw myself back on that horse pretty damn quick.'

'Is that an order?'

'I'm interested in how fast you do it,' Timms explained.

He rid himself of his dead birds. Not his firearm.

'I'll go when Laurel tells me to,' Jim announced. 'And if that's what she wants.'

Timms lifted his rifle skyward, squinting along the sights and working its bolt.

'I have a habit of leaving a shot up the spout,' he explained. 'That way, accidents happen. Especially to bystanders.'

'You got one in mind?' Jim asked.

'I just might,' Timms said. 'The kind aiming to come between husband and wife.'

Jim was silent.

'Laurel?' Timms said.

Laurel was frozen.

'Tell him to leave,' Timms ordered.

Her lips moved soundlessly.

'Come on,' he said.

Her gaze moved from Timms and back to Jim. 'Perhaps you'd best go,' she said.

'Hear that, Bird?' Timms said with satisfaction.

'I hear a frightened woman,' Jim said.

Timms lowered his rifle until it was trained at Jim's abdomen. The safety catch was off.

'And I'm seeing no more than a frightened man,' Jim added.

He waited for Timm's trigger finger to tighten. It failed to. Timms could still be relied on for second thoughts. Possibly he was considering the legalities of letting daylight into Jim: of how a plea of self-defence would hold up in court. Laurel would be undependable under oath. Witnesses willing to testify to his exemplary character might also be difficult to locate.

Without acknowledging danger, Jim turned to his horse, offering Timms his back as a target.

'Think yourself lucky this time,' Timms suggested. 'You won't be again. Mess with my marriage and you dig your bloody grave.'

'I daresay,' Jim said. 'I never met a man more expert in filling them.'

He didn't look over his shoulder, not even when he heard feet hard behind. It wasn't Timms. It was defiant Laurel, likely to inflame matters further. Astonished by her audacity, Timms seemed unable to do more than look on.

'You see how things are,' she whispered to Jim.

Jim nodded, his mouth dry.

'There isn't time to be modest,' she went on. 'I have to be brazen.'

'Go on,' he said, breathless. Timms hadn't rested his rifle; he could train it again.

'Remember my friend Betty Greenslade along the road? Write care of her. She has no love for my husband.'

Nor, it now went without saying, did Laurel.

'What is it you're asking me?' he said.

'To wait,' she whispered. 'I'll come when I can. Find somewhere to go.'

'To go?' Jim said, not comprehending.

'Somewhere well away.'

'For who?'

'Me,' she said. 'You.'

Jim's heart gave a heave.

'Just give me a call,' he said. 'Make it a loud one.'

Later that summer he began looking over the Coromandel.

I had been dozing. Alice was still distinctly awake.

'There,' she said. 'We've let it breathe.'

'It never hurts to give a good red an airing,' I said.

'Who's talking wine?' she asked.

'I thought you were,' I said.

'You're more of a drunk than I thought,' she decided.

'So what are we talking about?'

'The story,' she reminded me. 'Letting it breathe.'

'So we were,' I said vaguely.

'Your silences worry me,' she said. 'Are you sure you're not sickening for something?'

'It's almost midnight,' I pointed out.

'All right,' she said. 'I imagine the story, having been let off the leash, and had its little walk, will be the better for it tomorrow.'

That was possible. On the other hand I was aware that Alice didn't have many tomorrows.

'I imagine you're still wondering how the Coromandel fits in.'

'Now that you've got him there,' I admitted.

'Jim Bird was in no hurry either,' she said. 'Otherwise this narrative would be of no interest.'

'I'll take your word for it,' I said.

'You have no choice,' she observed.

'Did Jim Bird?'

'I imagine not,' she said.

'And Laurel?'

'Even less.'

Jim Bird's third encounter with the Coromandel, around 1906, didn't run true to form. This time he didn't disappear as summer cooled. The few on the peninsula familiar with his movements became aware that he had finished playing troglodyte in old mine entrances and set up something resembling permanent residence in Grief Gully. A two-room cottage of pit-sawn kauri, roofed with corrugated iron, it fell short of elegant. The interior, even more humble, was papered, New Zealand outback style, with the pictorial pages of *The Auckland Weekly*. He had also cleared and burned off enough scrub to sow grass and run livestock. There was nothing especially eccentric in that. There was, however, in the track he cleared into his territory. It frequently and inventively doubled back on itself; it was literally a maze, allowing Jim to view strangers before they sighted him. To complicate matters more, bulky trees had been felled across trails neighbouring his woodland retreat. Signs sprouted here and there with messages like *Not This Way* or *Go Back* or *Hazard Ahead*. Even veterans of the Coromandel highland could find themselves bushed. None had never seen a track so needlessly serpentine. A two-hour hike now took four, if it didn't finish in frustration. Those who did survive the maze met up with a rough sign saying: *Property of D. Smith. Shout and Identify Yourself on Approach*. Such a shout usually produced Jim, with a pipe in his mouth and a shotgun over his arm. He was seldom downright unfriendly. On the other hand he didn't make life comfortable for barefaced snoopers.

'It's like a bloody fortress,' one pig-hunter said, after accidentally breaching Jim's bachelor realm. Nevertheless he too reported Jim in amiable mood; Jim seldom let bona fide visitors leave without refreshment and a yarn. His home brew was judged the best on the peninsula. His yarns were reckoned as frothy. Still known as Dave Smith, he made himself memorable by reciting the ballads of Jim Bird, the popular rural wordsmith whose disappearance after the Boer war promised to become a lasting riddle, puzzled over at a thousand firesides. None of Dave Smith's listeners, not even those who fancied they knew him, suspected that the companion pouring beer might be the missing minstrel of the outback.

His visits to the town were few and infrequent. His calls were predictable: to the post office, pub, store and bank. His first was the post office. There he picked up letters addressed in a woman's hand; there he mailed letters addressed in his own rugged scrawl. At the pub he picked up bottles of his favoured malt whisky. At the store he collected staple provisions — flour, sugar, tobacco and tea — for a fortnight ahead. At the bank he traded in flakes of recently won gold for the currency of the realm. Gossip said he seldom did more than win wages from old workings on and around his property; he was no picture of affluence. On the other hand he wasn't heard complaining.

The point is, perhaps, that Jim Bird still didn't make sense; not after three years. Townfolk began to surmise that there might be more of a story to Jim than they earlier supposed. Some went further. They argued heartbreak. Jim was a good-looking, clean-cut and highly marriageable fellow. There was surely a woman in his past, perhaps still in the picture. Around 1907 those of that view could congratulate themselves on their prescience. A nomadic and notoriously unlucky prospector known as Dire Dick, passing Grief Gully, noted frilly feminine attire drying outside Jim's spartan dwelling. Where had it come from, and who was the woman? And how in hell had Jim smuggled her up there with none on the peninsula knowing? Anyway Dire Dick reported no female in the flesh; there were just those feminine items dancing in the breeze alongside Jim's manly flannel shirts. After damping down his thirst with Jim's latest brew, though not his curiosity, Dire Dick hiked on. His communique, however, revived interest in the squire of Grief Gully. For the next month Jim suffered several more visitors than normal, five or six rather than the customary two or three. They left thwarted. Unlike Dire Dick, they didn't spy anything out of the ordinary on Jim's washing line. Was Dick imagining things? Grief Gully was an unlikely location for a woman. It was unthinkable that any female would last long among dour forest, dangerous mineshafts and mist. One or two of his visitors were left with lingering suspicion. They noted that Jim had been busy again as a bush carpenter, making his cottage more durable. The lean-to at the rear had become larger and leak-proof, a more comfortable kitchen. They also reported that Jim seldom invited visitors inside; he entertained them on his porch or around an outdoor fire; they were lucky to be offered a sawn-log seat. This tended to support Dire Dick's view that there were ambiguous goings-on in Grief Gully.

Months passed, and much of a year. Jim's trips to town remained regular, offering little to the inquisitive. His wants at the pub, store and bank remained much the same. (Not until later was his purchase of sweet sherry, new on his shopping list, seen as significant. Cigarettes might also have been judged suspicious; Jim had never been seen smoking anything aside from an aged pipe. Boxes of chocolate also became apparent among his purchases. This was inconsistent with his frugal regime. If the luxury was noticed, it may have been presumed that Jim had lately developed a sweet tooth.) The one large change was that he had less use for the post office. One and one might have made two, with sherry, cigarettes and chocolate making five, but no one was counting. Then, on a spring day, a fussy and fidgety ex-schoolmaster and amateur ornithologist by name of Bandy Higgs, attempting to tally surviving native birdlife on the Coromandel, managed to miss Jim Bird's warning signs — even his artful zig-zag track — and tumbled into a bush clearing where a modest dwelling stood. The muddied arrival was amazed to find something passing for civilisation high in the hills. Sheep grazed fenced acres; a cow wandered in the company of two or three horses; there were flourishing flowerbeds and a nourishing vegetable garden. The man and a woman on view were as bemused as he. No drab farmwife in smoky apron, she was costumed neck to ankle in the manner of the last years of the old century or the first of the new. Her companion on the other hand made no concession to the fashion of any century: his notion of decent dress seldom amounted to more than a shapeless hat tipped back on his head, patched moleskins, grubby waistcoat and grimy boots. At that moment — though interloper Higgs wasn't to know it and was better oblivious — Jim Bird was deciding whether to reach for a firearm. After scrutinising bare-legged and bespectacled Higgs for some seconds he decided it unnecessary; he had never seen a man less menacing. The woman, meanwhile, fled indoors. There was a bang of door, then silence.

'Where'd you be from, then?' Jim Bird asked.

Higgs explained. He soon had Jim's attention.

'Birds?' Jim said. 'You're looking for birds?'

'For natives of all kinds and colours,' Higgs said breathlessly. 'The heights of the Coromandel have long been a paradise for the feathered, especially for those menaced by introduced species, predators carelessly allowed into the country, and of course man. This has become a sanctuary for many a species — from the frisky little fantail to the fat and lumbering wood pigeon. Even the beleaguered kiwi, despite its flightless state, grubs the forest floor by the score. Not to speak of equally earthbound parrots romping around. They remind us that this was a land empty of man, even of the lowliest mammal, populated only by birds. None of a commonplace sort either. All unique.' Higgs grew confidential. 'Furthermore,' he went on, his voice dropping to a whisper, 'there may be even more to this place.'

'More?' Jim queried. 'It sounds to me if you've got enough on your plate.'

'I speak of a creature perhaps lost, but not yet forgotten. In short, the huia. Above all, the huia. Yes.'

He waited for Jim to be awed.

'The huia?' Jim asked. 'Here?'

Though the creature had once figured in a Jim Bird ballad, he really knew no more of the species than its rarity. Its existence, if any, was now the stuff of lore.

'The huia,' Higgs confirmed. His voice didn't rise above a whisper; he looked over his shoulder as if fearful of eavesdroppers. 'As you possibly know, it is by far the most ravishing of New Zealand birds. Many suppose it extinct, now only to be seen preserved in museums. It may be. It may not. The fact is that I suspect it may survive in these ranges.'

'On what evidence?' Jim asked.

'That of my ears. The fact of the matter is that I fancy I have heard its song. Not just fancy. I *know* I've heard it.'

The fellow was too excitable by far.

'Here?' Jim said.

'On my honour,' Bandy insisted. 'It gives out, as all the books say, a sweet, wistful and most distinctive whistle. Some self-styled experts argue that the Coromandel is outside its range, too far north of its traditional habitat. I believe I shall prove otherwise. I suspect that some may have migrated here when man's fires drove them from their old breeding grounds. I like to imagine that some astute cock, sensitive to peril, led his loved hen away from danger and into safety; such a fellow might have seen a future here now that mankind has done its worst. Why not? Anyway its most fascinating feature is the fact that male and female not only have different appearances; they also have disparate functions. It appears to be the only species of bird in the world in which male and female have different beaks. That makes it one of God's more playful masterpieces.'

'You reckon?' Jim said, still less than overwhelmed.

'Indeed I do,' Higgs said 'The female's beak was — or is — long, slender and gracefully curved in sickle shape. The male's is stouter, blunt, and smaller. Devoted to his mate, he is the provider of little delicacies. His beak works as a pick-axe, bashing rotten logs apart and letting light in on fat grubs. With her elegant beak the female then dines daintily on the treats he furnishes. Males eat modestly, their diet limited to lesser insects; the choicest are for their mates. In return females caress their companions frequently, with affectionate twitters. Their lives seem to be a long idyll. Not surprisingly, they are monogamous. The hen, for one, is never tempted to stray; she knows which side her bread is buttered — or, should I say, which grubs are sauced with the sweat of her lover.'

'You've given this creature a lot of thought,' Jim concluded.

'I encounter it often in dream,' Higgs confessed. 'For the Maori it was the most spiritual of birds; its feathers were prized above all others and reserved for the trimming of chieftain's cloaks. Men of rank were buried with huia feathers bedecking their heads. Their decorative character hastened its decline in numbers before European man began shooting them out of the trees. They were esteemed as a sweet-fleshed pioneer delicacy. Others, after a taxidermist had finished with them, went to collectors prepared to pay large prices. That disgusting trade is believed to have put an end to them. Who is to say? Not me. It's just possible that you too have heard its honeymoon call here, with no awareness of what you were hearing.'

'Maybe,' Jim grunted. 'The fact of the matter is that I've had more on my mind than birds.'

'All the same,' Higgs said, 'I'd be grateful if you kept an eye out. And an ear free. Bird watching needs no large skills. Just patience.'

'I expect I could give it a go,' Jim said in improved humour. 'Who knows? I could turn out to have the knack for it, the knack and the name.'

That left Higgs baffled. 'Your meaning escapes me,' he said.

'Never mind,' Jim Bird said. 'I'll tell you one day.'

'In the event that you come up with a reliable sighting, I shall ensure you receive credit for the find.'

'That won't be necessary,' Jim said.

'Oh?' said Higgs.

'I don't need my name in the newspapers. Nor people trampling around.'

'I see,' Higgs said. 'But you don't object to me?'

'Should I?' Jim said.

He considered his fervent visitor for a moment longer. Then he ambled to his dwelling and opened the door. 'Laurel?' he could be heard saying. 'Laurel? It's all right. You can come out now. We're going to entertain our first real visitor. He looks like he could do with a drop of tea. Maybe a slice of your fruit cake too.'

Laurel's call, when it finally came, had been more than just the despondent cry he was three years awaiting. It was worse than his ugliest expectation. The first half of the letter informed him that old Mr Green had died, that his farm was now on the market. Laurel and her brothers had agreed on selling, though Laurel's husband, seeing a lucrative situation slip from his grasp, had vehemently not been party to the decision. Jim skipped much of this. What Timms wanted, or didn't, was of no interest. The important thing was that with her father dead, the farm for sale, Laurel was now free of everything but marriage. And regardless of what the law said, or the church, it was a marriage made on deceit. In that respect conscience wasn't going to cost Jim a night's sleep.

The second half of the letter dimmed his elation. Laurel was writing from a hospital bed. She had been the victim of a mysterious assault, one the police were investigating with no success. Handicapped by Laurel's loss of memory, the aftermath of concussion, they were in search of some homicidal itinerant, some nameless stranger, not someone nearer home. Her face had been battered; she had been left with broken ribs. An especially vindictive blow to her midriff had brought on a miscarriage. Jim, she said, was not to panic; she was feeling better already. But could he come, and soon?

Jim could. Before the day was out he was pushing a horse north with two other horses roped in his wake: one a packhorse and the other saddled and ready for a rider. Strapped to his own saddle was a rifle useful for bringing down pig and goat, rabbit and duck. A nameless stranger? He could suggest a name, even if Laurel couldn't or loyally wouldn't.

'Mrs Laurel Timms?' he asked at the hospital, though he had difficulty getting his tongue around the surname without a tremor.

The duty nurse consulted a file. 'Mrs Timms was taken home by her husband yesterday,' she informed Jim. 'Discharged and returned home.'

'By her husband?'

'That is correct.'

'Dear God,' he said.

'Is something wrong?' the nurse asked.

Jim was already out the door.

He waited on dusk before approaching the homestead. When lamps were lit and curtains drawn, he led the three horses furtively uphill. A faint moon lit the terrain. He seemed to be on a stealthy night trek through Boer territory, with the slightest clink of harness likely to draw bullets. Finally he tethered the horses, unsheathed his rifle, and continued afoot. When his boots encountered the verandah, dogs began barking. Within the homestead there was a familiar voice.

'What the hell is that?' Timms was saying.

Jim gave Timms no time to conduct a reconnaissance. He found the front door unlocked and kicked it open. Then he pushed into the homestead. A log fire burned in the living room. The evening meal had been finished. Timms sat in an armchair, pipe in hand, a newspaper on his knee. Laurel was clearing the table, collecting soiled dishes.

Timms was quick to his feet. Laurel turned stiffly, her face slow coming into view. It was still scarred and discoloured, and must have been worse.

Timms failed to express himself coherently.

'Fetch your belongings,' Jim told Laurel.

'I'm ready,' she said. Out of trance, if still too feeble to smile, she limped off to the rear of the house.

Timms seemed about to move too. He changed his mind when Jim used the rifle to prod him in the belly. 'Sit down,' Jim advised. 'No one has to be hurt. And especially not Laurel. She's damaged enough.'

Timms sat reluctantly.

'I suppose you think you know everything,' he said.

'I've tasted your knuckles too,' Jim pointed out.

Timms was silent.

Jim explained, 'If you follow us tonight we just might ride to the nearest constable. Laurel just might make a statement about who did her hurt. If I were you, I'd think hard on that.'

Timms showed some inclination to think, if joylessly.

'With your war record, it's possible that a magistrate might take a compassionate view,' Jim added. 'On the other hand the medical evidence wouldn't be pretty.'

Timms appeared to choke.

'Do you think you'll get away with it?' he said. 'Do you think I'll let this end here?'

'Funny you should mention it,' Jim said. 'I had a feeling you mightn't.'

'It's a small country,' Timms persisted.

'We'll take our chances on that.'

Laurel returned with belongings bundled. Jim, still with an eye on Timms, was alarmed. 'Enough,' he pleaded. 'You can't take everything.'

'It's mostly sentimental things and clothes,' she protested.

'Just take your good outfits. Your old won't last.' He added, 'Better we take the household rifle too. Your husband might be tempted to make matters worse.'

Timms wasn't inclined to wait on temptation. Nor had he need of a weapon. The moment he imagined Jim off guard he launched himself powerfully at the pair, his head low and his fists swinging. Laurel was crashed aside as he made for Jim. Having rehearsed this eventuality all the long ride north, Jim was ready and efficient. He brought the butt of his rifle up under Timms' jaw. Then, reversing the weapon, he whipped its barrel across Timms' skull. The crack of metal on bone was impressive. The encounter ended with his former superior dazed, groping, and feeble on the floor. There was blood from a broken lip and facial bruises beginning to swell and darken. Spluttering, Timms finally spat teeth. At first Jim was shocked by the satisfaction he felt. Qualms didn't last. Nothing put the world to rights faster than revenge proficiently consummated.

'There wasn't need for this to be messy,' he told Timms.

Timms didn't hear. He slumped back to the floor, cradling his head in his arms and shedding more blood.

Jim was fast into the night, with Laurel following; her possessions were strapped to the packhorse, Timms' rifle too. Timms, discovering his feet, staggered out on to the verandah, bellowing obscenities.

'I'll have your balls yet,' he warned. 'Your tits too, you bitch.'

It was still possible that Timms might take them apart — if not with a knife, then with knowledge of the law. Jim was unsure of his ground in that respect. He, not Timms, might finish in a cell. Some chances weren't worth taking.

Next morning Timms' confiscated rifle was resident in a roadside ditch. The Green homestead was also a generous distance behind. Was Timms? And if so, how far? If not, how near? Laurel was not to be rushed; she had to be nursed. Safety was slow coming. They preferred clay byways to gravel highways, obscure tracks to frequented bridle paths. On the second day Laurel began bleeding. The third day was worse. Jim took her to a township doctor. The doctor's face was unhappy. He took Jim aside. 'This woman has barely survived what seems a vicious assault,' he observed. 'Should the authorities be informed, or is it not my business?'

'It's not your business,' Jim decided.

'I'd like her in hospital for observation,' the doctor said. 'She may have serious internal injury. At the least she shouldn't travel.'

Jim put this to Laurel.

'Fetch the horses,' she said.

Auckland lay across their route south; Jim counted on it being a barrier to Timms after they crossed it. So it was. With the city behind, it was less difficult to relax. They no longer ate cold food quickly; they lingered beside their roadside fires. Laurel's bleeding stopped as incomprehensibly as it had begun. After a dozen slow days and more than a hundred miles on the move they saw Coromandel heights covered thinly with cloud. Light rain freshened their faces.

'That's it?' she asked.

'Home,' he promised.

He looked to their rear. There was no horseman in near view. Nor, for that matter, in far.

Next morning, as eastern sky paled, the couple might have been seen cantering through the township and toward the hills. They were not seen. It was months before it became common knowledge that Dave Smith no longer lived alone. He still rode down to the town often enough. His companion never did. They thought it wise not to be seen together. Though she may not have realised it, not at first, this meant she had as good as said farewell to the world. She was in a neighbourhood without neighbours. No woman would live there from choice, and not many men. It would be years before Laurel sighted others of her sex. That was no reason to discontinue prayers of a heartfelt sort. She would have liked a church, a clerical blessing. She didn't mourn for much else. There wasn't much else to be mourned.

I woke, confused, after a short break from the world.

'Well?' Alice sighed. 'Still in the land of the living, are we?'

'You might be,' I said. 'I'm having second thoughts.'

'What's your complaint this time?'

'Your easy-going approach to narrative. I see another long night.'

'Good God,' she said. 'Where's your backbone?'

With my fatigue unworthy of further discussion, she wrong-footed me with a sly shift of subject.

'I note,' she continued, 'that you have hardly been out of the house lately. Also that you have been keeping virtuous hours. It must be a week since you last quarrelled with my furniture.'

'Possibly,' I said.

'There have also been refreshingly few telephone calls. And, when there have been, no troubled female at the other end.'

'That had escaped me,' I claimed.

'It certainly hasn't escaped *me,*' she said. 'Moreover I cannot help noting that there has been a dramatic drop in the contents of my whisky bottle.'

'That could be coincidental,' I suggested.

'It could,' she said. 'It might also confirm that there has been some serious tippling under my roof. Solo drinking at that, quite the worst kind.'

'I'm sorry,' I said finally. 'I'll replace it tomorrow.'

'My missing whisky isn't the point,' she said.

'So what is?'

'If you're going to be an alcoholic, make a job of it. Don't fiddle about. There's nothing more nauseating than a half-hearted drunk.'

'I'll work on it,' I promised.

'And by the way, should you decide to shake me off too, I trust that I receive fair warning.'

'Naturally,' I agreed.

'More conviction would be in order.'

'All right, then. I promise not to head for the hills until I know whether Timms caught up with Jim and Laurel.'

'One other thing,' she said. 'Before you drink yourself to death you might give that woman friend of yours a call.'

'What for?'

'I need a rest. Playing Scheherazade isn't my idea of a good night out. Also your former companion deserves a decent apology. Perhaps even a candlelit dinner. Use the extension phone in your bedroom if you prefer me not to eavesdrop.'

I did this with reluctance. Some fraught minutes later I returned to Alice.

'Well?' she asked. 'Better?'

'Let's say no one was hurt,' I told her.

'Good,' she said briskly. 'So where are we?'

'In 1907,' I suggested. 'Perhaps 1908.'

'I don't mean dates. I mean *where*.'

'Desirably where the favoured few live happily ever after.'

'As you well know, only fairytale princesses and pumpkins live happily ever after, no doubt due to their celibate condition.'

'Why pick on pumpkins?' I asked.

'Have you ever met an unhappy pumpkin?' she said.

More weeks went, more months, then years. No undesirable put in an appearance. Others did, principally bird-loving Bandy. Unimpressed by evidence to the contrary, he continued to persuade himself that a clandestine huia duet might be heard in the Coromandel's heart. Meanwhile he made do with sightings of lesser species, sometimes flightless, often unattractively tuneless. His enthusiasm won Jim and Laurel over; they joined him in his search. Jim's familiarity with the terrain was especially useful. To win vantage points in the forest, he climbed trees which ungainly Bandy was unwilling to chance. Laurel, on the other hand, possessed a sensitive ear, with eyes quite as keen. The pursuit of refugee songsters may have helped fill any lack they may have felt in their lives. ('Lack?' I asked Alice. 'Children,' she said.) When Bandy was absent, they kept scrupulous record of likely birdsong and its location. Grief Gully became their personal aviary. Some birds became individuals, regular visitors, with names. All fed on the crusts of home-baked bread Laurel scattered from the door of their dwelling; they skittered in the bird baths Jim arranged for their entertainment. Since their door was often left open, Jim and Laurel, on returning from a late afternoon hike, were never surprised to find a bold creature in residence, pecking up crumbs. Such pampering did not meet with Bandy's unqualified approval. Birds were best observed *in situ*, where God placed them in the world's morning. In the end, though, Bandy let this scruple lapse. Laurel and Jim, *in situ* themselves, were too precious as friends. When Bandy visited, Jim gave up on gold for the day and Laurel abandoned her baking. With Laurel's scones for sustenance, the trio rose early, long before first light, and wormed their way into shadowy forest. There they were rewarded with intemperate bursts of melody. But never, or not positively, with a sound said to put lovebirds to shame — the male huia's randy whistle backed by his paramour's coquettish twitters.

If Bandy wasn't about, Laurel and Jim walked the forest on their own account. That was how they happened on the eccentric frogs of the Coromandel. Tame and freakishly tiny, they squatted on Jim's thumbnail without a flicker of fright. Ingeniously, or so he learned from Bandy, these unconventional creatures saw no point in beginning as tadpoles; they renounced the convoluted antics of their gross cousins. At dusk there were other originals, tiny bush bats beginning their rounds, the only mammals who could call New Zealand home. And lizards. And owls with their rhythmic and seemingly carnivorous cry of *morepork, morepork*.

It is time to draw the curtains on idyll; time for a infusion of that gritty realism Alice despised. How did Jim and Laurel live? How, that is, did they manage? The question has to be asked; it also has to be answered. To call their life austere doesn't meet the case. Their existence was more than lean. Unlike many in the depression years to come, they never lacked food on their table, a roof overhead. But electricity never lit their lives, eased their chill, or cooked their food. Nor was there piped water. It had to be carried from the creek where the weekly wash was done. No telephone pealed in their hearing. The catalogue of their lacks was large. The one prized item of technology in the cottage was Laurel's foot-powered sewing machine. Her original wardrobe had grown threadbare. Laurel was not one to let standards slump; the sewing machine became her ally in the wilderness. Jim fetched samples of material from the town draper and Laurel made her selection. He would revisit the draper with her chosen sample and make the desired purchase. On his return her busy feet pumped out a new dress. These were invariably long and flowing with never a nod in the direction of the 20th century. She knew nothing of contemporary fashions. Such as she saw of them, illustrated murkily in the newspapers which wrapped their groceries, didn't persuade her to change.

After two decades they had a cast-iron stove fuelled with wood.

That, on cold Coromandel nights, was more to the point.

They had a covenant with gold. It was Jim's belief that too much might cost them their equilibrium, with avarice begetting frustration. Not to be tempted, they uplifted only such as they needed for survival, harvesting it from hillsides, old tailings, tree roots, lumps of Coromandel quartz, and the residues of river and stream. This was laborious and seldom enriching. According to Jim's calculation there was sufficient in their vicinity to see out their lifetimes so long as they didn't let it go to their heads. Most narratives of gold-seeking, fiction or fact, are threaded with lust and doom. For the most part the reality was more benign. *Gold is the great friend of the masses*, said the campfire song. It often did more for the humble than politicians, reformers or revolutionaries. It let harassed workmen say goodbye to bosses, impecunious farm labourers to become farmers, paupers to prosper as publicans. It also permitted runaway lovers to survive. For such as Laurel and Jim, foraging in the rearguard of the rushes, gold was never more than a workaday business, without theatricals, with seldom an excited shout. 'A clear head begets sharp eyes,' he told her.

His cockiness, however, diminished after Laurel's arrival. He wanted to show Laurel what he was about on his long hikes from home. He also hoped to train her eyes; a helpmate wouldn't hurt. With a geologist's hammer he chipped promising lumps of quartz as they walked, passing fragments over for her inspection. Eventually she became impatient with Jim's long lectures on the capricious nature of gold in auriferous or alluvial form. Raising her skirts, she roamed off alone among rock and weed.

'Here,' she called, barely five minutes gone.

'What?' he asked.

Laurel was kneeling. 'I've found some,' she claimed.

'It'll be fool's gold,' he announced with confidence. 'Iron pyrites. I should have warned you. It tricks all of us at first.'

He joined her, nevertheless, hammer in hand.

'See?' she said. 'There.'

Jim looked, condescendingly, and saw a thin gush of water,

deriving from recent rain, undercutting a bluff. At its foot, checked by rock, fine debris shone. Gold? Jim raised his hammer with the intention of chipping away surplus rock to view things better. Her hand halted him.

'This needs a woman's touch,' she argued.

She unpinned a handsome antique brooch, in the shape of a sword, from her costume. 'My mother's,' she explained. 'It might just be lucky.' She used the unlikely tool to investigate the crevice from which the water came. While Jim watched nonplussed, yellow specks swam free.

'See?' Laurel said.

He couldn't fail to.

'My God,' he said.

With a surgeon's delicacy, Laurel continued to make more probes with her toy-sized sabre, freeing more gold from the ground. Jim joined in the hunt in a more conventional manner, with trowel and pan. At the end they were wealthier by a good ounce of gold, enough for a burst of luxury in their lives.

Jim never mentioned fool's gold again. The story of Laurel's triumph over traditional technique, with a few swings of her silver sword, might have gone well in a Jim Bird ballad. Not that it did.

'Beginners' luck,' he grumbled.

There was further humiliation.

'You should learn to use my rifle,' he said.

For what?' she asked.

'For emergency,' he replied. He was not disposed to be precise. 'For the days when I'm in town. For prowlers perhaps. An overhead shot can work wonders.'

'I don't see the need,' she protested.

'You might,' he insisted. 'Come on. Time for your first lesson.'

He led her outdoors, rifle in hand, and set a tin can on a fence post. Rudimentary instruction followed. Then, down to business, he sighted their rifle on the can. 'The important thing,' he explained, 'is to think your bullet into the target.'

'Think?' she said.

'If you fancy the bullet finding your target, as often as not it will.'

'Show me,' she said.

He fired. The can rocked slightly in the wind of his shot. It didn't fall. It was also undamaged.

'See that as a lesson too,' he said. 'Not many hit the target every time. And never the first time out. Don't be discouraged.'

She took the rifle gingerly and trained it with care. 'Just imagine the bullet hitting clean in the centre,' he urged. 'Think it as hard as you can.'

She fired. The punctured can leapt from the post. As shots went, it couldn't have been cleaner.

'Bloody hell,' Jim whispered with awe.

'Did I do something wrong?' she asked innocently.

'Nothing,' he said, at a loss.

'I just did what you said,' she pointed out. 'I thought the bullet into the target.'

'I saw that,' he said.

'I won't be so lucky next time,' she predicted.

She was, though, and three times out of five. The most he could manage was one demolished can after four attempts to harm it.

'It must be my eyesight,' he decided.

'Or mine,' she said.

'Maybe,' he said tersely.

'Mind you,' she said, 'I had an excellent tutor.'

'There's nothing I can teach you,' he decided.

Jim, however, had known more chivalrous days.

As exiles they remained in luck. Census takers failed to find them; they were never numbered as citizens. Save for Jim's discharge from the army, there wasn't a document testifying to the existence of either. An inland revenue inspector, hearing rumour of tax evaders in the hills, set out to locate them. He was found with a broken leg and half-dead of exposure. Yet the world beyond was never quite banished. One dusk Laurel raced into the cottage with startling information.

'A star has just dropped from the sky,' she reported.

She raced Jim outside to witness the universe unravel. At first sight her claim seemed to have substance. Somewhere beyond tree and sea, where no star shone before, a lone light moved mysteriously.

She shivered. Jim laughed. 'It's a car, not a star,' he announced. 'A car, with lights, on the new coast road.'

That, trivially, was that. More lights, in the months following, could be seen traversing the new road. Until they became commonplace, Laurel watched the moving lights nightly and tried to imagine the travellers nested in the vehicles. Entire families perhaps, women and children. Bearded grandfathers, grandmothers bent to their knitting, and boisterous babies. People. She concealed her desperation from Jim, if not always well. Though death certificates never acknowledge it, loneliness can kill. With a surfeit of silence men and women wither. They need a mix of human voices, the small change of the seasons. They need even the nothings of gossip. Jim wasn't a fountain of small talk. Nothing in and around Grief Gully was news. That made surprise more precious.

The next shock romped in from clear sky. Jim was off prospecting useful pockets of quartz for his crusher, leaving Laurel alone. First there was a faint sound beyond the hills, barely more than the noise of a bee. Then it was monstrous. With a rising roar and a rush of air, more bewitching than anything she dreamed, a biplane swooped overhead, all but clipping treetops. Laurel, in her flower garden, found herself waving with passion. The pilot, in his tight leather helmet, with goggles shielding his eyes, could have been a caller from a far planet. Below his goggles was a trim moustache, a toothy smile, and a fluttering silk scarf. He returned her wave with enthusiasm. Possibly he was as astonished. An elegantly garbed woman alone in a forest clearing was an unexpected find on a joyride. To take a second look, the aviator adjusted his goggles, put the aircraft into a steep turn, and soared back to Laurel; he whipped off his scarf and gallantly let it trail in his slipstream. Then hazardous hilltops made him climb higher and out of view.

By the time Jim arrived home the pilot was adventuring elsewhere.

'What was that sod up to?' Jim asked dourly. He had read of aeroplanes and seen photographs. That didn't mean he welcomed one around Grief Gully.

'He was just being friendly,' Laurel argued. 'He waved to me. I waved back.'

'You *waved* to him?' Jim said with incredulity. '*Waved?*'

'And why not?'

'You don't know who the bugger could be. He could be anyone.'

Anyone meant someone. That someone could be Timms or a hireling. Aircraft made Grief Gully less a secret. Their sanctuary was open for anyone to see.

All the same, Jim's anger didn't last. 'You weren't to think,' he said charitably. 'I might have lost my head myself.'

'You?' she said, and laughed.

'Stranger things have happened,' he argued.

Laurel was left with guilt and elation. She had been more than just careless. In allowing herself to be courted by a winged Casanova, she felt she had been disloyal too. It was a week before dreams of an airborne nature allowed her to meet Jim's eye. Though she desired no other companion, their union wasn't easy. She wished Jim less himself. A bachelor before her arrival, he looked a bachelor still. In the long evenings, with his pipe and whisky, he was comfortable with silences of the sort she found oppressive. The harmless quirks which attach to solitaries were hardening into unsociable habits; his armchair grunts were those of a man who communicated mainly with himself. There were times when she wondered what his need of her was. Whatever it had been, whatever it might be still, it was nothing that might be mistaken as flighty; Jim never had his head in the clouds. Nor was he likely to lose it.

In their first years nights were reserved for reading. In yellow lamplight, through increasingly ancient spectacles, Jim nourished himself on the red meat of Jack London and Joseph Conrad, sometimes with side-dishes of Dickens. Laurel's reading was of a less robust kind. She preferred the moors of Emily Bronte, while her tame Heathcliff, with sleeves rolled, sat broody nearby. On the whole, though, she favoured verse above fiction. Tennyson and Christina Rosseti were her poets, and lately Rupert Brooke. They were less to Jim's taste. 'The buggers take too long to get to the point,' he complained.

Jim wasn't indifferent to Laurel's loneliness, to the pains of an unpeopled life. For much of their time Bandy Higgs was the best they had for company, the closest they had to a confidante. (He was also a proficient referee when one or other of them, or both, had the sulks.) Bandy was the first on the Coromandel to establish Jim's identity. This happened when Jim lent him Gibbons' *Decline and Fall* in all five volumes. Within one of these volumes, functioning as a bookmark, were several stanzas of verse in the hand of the man Bandy had until then known as Dave Smith. They weren't the liveliest lines Jim Bird had written in his heyday; on the other hand the erratic rhymes meant there was no mistaking their author. Bandy had been a reader of New Zealand's back country bard before the latter put away his pen.

'So you aren't Dave Smith,' Bandy said with no preliminary as they walked the forest.

'I don't know what you're talking about,' Jim claimed.

'Come on,' Bandy said. 'Admit you're Jim Bird and I won't tell.'

'Do you need to know?' Jim asked.

'I do,' Bandy said. 'I can't speak for others.'

'I'd prefer that there were no others,' Jim explained. 'It might mean trouble. For Laurel too.'

'Come to think, 'Bandy said, 'I've never heard her surname.'

'Let it stay that way,' Jim asked.

'Fair's fair,' Bandy said. 'Just one thing, though. What happened to Jim Bird? What did he do right? Or wrong? Why did he disappear?'

'I never got around to asking him,' Jim said.

The chronic silences of Grief Gully diminished on the day Jim arrived back from town with a mysterious box and a queerly shaped parcel. 'Here,' he said gruffly. 'This should keep you quiet.'

'What will?' she said.

Jim gently removed wrapping. 'This,' he said, standing aside to let Laurel marvel.

She found it difficult to speak. She reached out, rather cautiously, to touch the gift. 'Is it what I think it is?' she asked.

'It is,' he confirmed. 'A gramophone.'

'With music?' she marvelled.

'I'll want my money back if there's none,' he told her.

The odd parcel proved to be a horn-shaped speaker. He attached the speaker to the box and cranked up the workings within. Then he fixed a needle to the arm of the apparatus and arranged a record with care. He had been two hours with a salesman rehearsing this moment; he didn't want their first concert flawed by incompetence.

'Ready?' he asked.

'Ready,' she said faintly.

She closed her eyes. The swelling music was from an opera, with a soprano voice floating overhead. Years later they were still arguing about whose aria, from whose opera, they heard first. 'Verdi's,' she claimed. 'Donizetti's,' he argued. Not that the names mattered then or later. Their music did.

'How did you know?' she asked. 'How did you know I loved opera?'

'A little bird whispered in my ear,' he said.

The fact was that she had told him years earlier. She, over the years, had forgotten. He hadn't.

'Anyway,' she declared, 'it carries me away.'

There was more in that confession than met the ear. They were up until midnight and after, until the last of Jim's job-lot of records had been played, some of them twice. There were few events more sensational in their lives.

By then, whatever Laurel's misgivings, it was plain that they were in Grief Gully to stay. Nothing, not even a vagrant pilot now, was likely to lift Laurel away. This was confirmed when her horse rolled on a greasy slope. Laurel went with her mount, her leg twisting under her. There was no mistaking the crack of bone. Though her discomfort was considerable, she remained stoic.

'We've got to get you down to the town,' Jim announced.

'Down?'

'To the doctor.'

'I am not,' she informed him, 'going to town.'

'Of course you are,' he replied. 'I can't set bone. You could be left crippled.'

Common sense, he imagined, should win. It didn't show itself fast.

'There'll be people,' she pointed out.

'People?'

'Staring and talking.'

'Maybe,' he admitted. 'But you can't expect them to hide their heads just because Lady Laurel's come to town at last. People staring and talking are the least of your worries. First things first. That means putting your leg together. A day or two in hospital. That's all.'

'Jim,' she said stubbornly, 'I am not going to town.'

'Why the bloody hell not?'

She shook her head. Though she couldn't tell Jim, she knew why. She feared that once she took a track out of the forest she might not stop; it mightn't be in her power to stop. Even with a damaged wing, a caged bird doesn't spurn an open door.

'Jim,' she pleaded, 'don't make me. Just cover me with a blanket. Then go for the doctor.'

They were more than a mile from home. Jim, often stumbling, carried her there. Her distress didn't lessen. He deposited her on a bed and covered her with a warm blanket. He also dosed her generously with whisky.

'I'll be back before dark,' he promised.

He was, and in company with a dishevelled young doctor. Kerosene lamps shed light on her injured limb. Examining her gently, the doctor suspected more than one crack in the bone.

'I should prefer to deal with you in my surgery,' he told Laurel.

'Out of the question,' she told him stiffly.

'Why ever not?' the doctor said.

'For one thing, young man, I never leave my husband alone. I most certainly have no intention of affording him the opportunity of running off with promiscuous women. Besides which he's inclined to poison himself with his own cooking. What if something happened to *him*?'

The doctor used chloroform to ease Laurel into sleep before rearranging bone and setting her leg in bulky plaster. With first light the doctor departed, his job efficiently done and Laurel arranged on cushions. Panic was past. They were alone again. She was still weak, and the chloroform left her hazy. Jim poured tea when she judged her stomach could hold it.

'I imagine I heard right,' he said.

'Heard what?'

'Heard you calling me husband.'

'It is entirely possible,' she said.

'Does that mean I call you wife?'

'I imagine it does.'

It was also possible that Laurel heard a door shut. But for Timms they were still in business. And for all they knew Timms might now be dead. Jim thought not to call attention to himself by making inquiries. Since he never read them, newspapers told him nothing. As for formal vows, neither of them fancied bigamy. Like it or not, Timms might remain her lawful husband for life.

The doctor was back to check on his handiwork. As obliging as ever, he brought along the town dentist; Laurel's untended teeth appeared to concern the conscientious doctor as much as her leg. 'We may save them,' the dentist reported, and managed to rescue all but a molar or two. 'How you managed, I don't care to imagine,' he added.

Laurel might have enlightened him. She had long ago learned to swallow pain, with whisky washing it down.

'There,' he said. 'All shipshape now.'

Forced to sit with her leg up, week after week, Laurel was denied most of a vivid spring. She didn't see the yellow flowers of the kowhai blooming or scores of parson-throated tui picking them apart for their nectar; she also missed wood-pigeon fattening with the berries of the puriri. Attentive Jim was seldom out of sight as she healed. If she wouldn't go to the world, the world might be brought to her. Jim packed a heavy cabinet up from the town.

Limping on a crutch, Laurel circled it slowly; Jim insisted that she guess what it was.

'I'll give you a clue,' he said. 'You don't have to wind this up.'

'A radio?' Laurel asked.

Rumour had told her of radio.

'Consider it a wedding present,' he informed her. 'You mightn't live long enough to get another.'

Next day he climbed a tree, a little creakily, and threaded a long wire back to the cottage and then to the cabinet itself. 'What is it for?' she asked.

'It's an aerial,' he explained. 'It works like a fishing line, hooking things from the air waves.'

'Air waves?

'Invisible waves carrying music and talk.' To prove it, Jim hitched two large batteries to the contrivance. He tripped a switch and a light began glowing. There was a pause, as if someone within the cabinet was drawing breath, and then a stranger's voice feebly entered the room. Jim turned a knob until the voice rose to comprehensible level. Laurel had to look over her shoulder to ensure that there was no third party present. All Jim told her about air waves was true.

She now had the company of distant voices nightly, sometimes speaking unfamiliar languages from a far quarter of the globe. As for music, the air waves washing around them meant there was less wear on their crackling records. Radio hadn't made their gramophone redundant. In good weather they carried it outdoors. There were some, Bandy Higgs among them, who suspected that music saved Laurel's sanity.

In 1948 Alice had an overpowering desire to view the Coromandel again, the locale of her infancy and youth. She had been considering such an excursion for decades, or approximately since her first husband died. If she didn't do it now, never was near. She took her daughters Jane and Lucy and seven lively grandchildren on a camping trip to the peninsula. There she found herself in thrall to a narrative which made hers lacklustre; her past was sidelined without ceremony.

In short, she encountered Jim Bird and the former Laurel Green.

'Hang on,' I said.

'Is something the matter?'

'You said 1948.'

'Indeed I did,' Alice said.

'It can't be,' I protested.

'And why not?'

'For one thing you've just mislaid forty years.'

'Not so I've noticed.'

'Come on,' I said. 'You were in 1908.'

'*You* may have been,' she said. 'Not, I think, me.'

'You can't skip forty years like that.'

'Why not?' she asked.

'Alice,' I said patiently, 'you appear to be telling me that Jim and Laurel hid out on the Coromandel for most of half a century.'

'At long last,' she said, 'you may be getting the point.'

'For half a century?'

'At least for half a lifetime. Then they found that, even with danger gone, they had little choice in the matter; that existence elsewhere was not to be contemplated, the world nowhere to be trusted. Also they knew where they were. The peninsula had been a means to an end. Then, as is often mysteriously the case, the means became the end.'

'With only barmy bird-watchers and addled old prospectors for company?'

'And Mad Matt.'

'Mad who?'

'Mad Matt.'

'Who would he be, then?'

'Their fractious Maori associate. Am I really so vague? Haven't I mentioned him?'

'Not in my hearing,' I said.

'Fancy that,' she sighed.

'Do I need to know about him?'

'Unless you are content to remain deprived,' she said.

'I can't see that a late addition to the cast is likely to make a difference. Their lives couldn't have been less eventful.'

'On one view of the matter.'

'Is there another? We're talking solitary confinement.'

It might be said that they were sufficient to themselves; that they had all the company they needed.'

'It might,' I conceded. 'But I don't hear you saying it.'

I had seen the gleam in Alice's eye.

'Possibly not,' she agreed.

'So you're telling me this Maori's important?'

'You may well conclude so,' she said.

'I'm not in a position to conclude anything until I know who he is. Or was.'

Neither Alice nor her narratives had much respect for chronology. Just when I seemed to glimpse light ahead, we were limping back to 1917.

The Maori arrived in their lives at the end of their first decade on the peninsula, three years after war began flashing along the world's horizons. This one made past conflicts, and not least colonial scuffles like the Boer war, seem petty. Momentous though it may have been, the news was slow finding a path through the growth enclosing Grief Gully. Jim Bird and Laurel Green may even have been the last New Zealanders to learn of it. For that matter there must have been few in the furthest reaches of the British Empire who remained oblivious as long. The guns had been discharging for months; Germany's Kaiser had begun dismembering Belgium. Armchair strategists were predicting a million casualties before the war's first year was out. It was also to the point that it been a cruelly wet winter, with the track out from Grief Gully perilously muddy. Jim, as storm followed gale, postponed a trip to town until the track became tolerable. It didn't. When lack of whisky finally persuaded him to risk the outdoors, he rode cautiously to town and there looked around with wonder. It seemed some sorcerer had been at work in the main street: there was hardly a man under forty to be seen. ('Like Hamelin after the Pied Piper's raid,' he reported to Laurel.) There were new faces in the bank, the store and the pub:

faces of elderly men out of retirement and of former housewives substituting for missing males. Jim sensed some natural disaster. Even Bandy had been spirited away; his cottage stood mysteriously empty. Twopence spent on a newspaper told Jim of the new war. Volunteers early to the colours were already seaborne, bound for Europe; there was patriotic agitation, sure to become noisier, for country-wide conscription to net cowards and outfit shirkers in khaki. Other lives were already disrupted. Bandy's, for example. He had returned to an Auckland classroom to free a young teacher to die in France.

Jim rode back to Grief Gully thoughtful. For three years that was about as much as he and Laurel had of the war. Jim saw no point in wasting further pence on newspapers fattened with casualty lists. Parents with black armbands, widows in veils, and soon young men limbless and sometimes mindless from the hilltops of Turkey and the mire of France, told him more than he needed to know. His trips to town, never numerous anyway, became brief. Contagion was abroad there. It was not something he wished to carry home to Laurel. And there was more of a toxic nature. Though Jim was no longer of an age for soldiering, his unlined face suggested otherwise to some. Tethering his horse to a town hitching post, he was moistened with the saliva of a middle-aged matron and presented with a white feather.

Then there was the Maori. The peninsula's first people were now thin on the ground and seldom seen upland at all. Some had followed dismantled sawmills south. Others once employed in corporate mines, found city jobs easier on the lungs. Matt, through no wish of his own, was the exception which doesn't prove rules.

Toward dusk on a warm spring day in 1917 Jim Bird was out on a solo stroll. It was his custom to shoulder his rifle and take a last look over his territory before nightfall, before locking the door of his dwelling against the world. It could be seen as a perfunctory form of picket duty, or as eccentric habit; they were surely past peril. Now that Bandy had given him an ear for it, he enjoyed forest evensong for itself, not just in hope of hearing the elusive huia. Even

Bandy, well before he went off to do his bit for the war, suspected that its silence was now everlasting.

On reaching a minor summit, Jim lit his pipe, looked around, and then turned for home. Then he saw a faint glow and wisping smoke. He pointed himself in that direction with care. Encounters with fellow humans in the ranges remained few, fewer with the passing years, and never to be expected with night near. For his peace of mind Jim needed to know who the outsider might be.

Minutes later he brushed aside fern and looked into a surprising domestic scene. In profile there was a rather dark, bulky and hairy fellow, too shadowy to be identifiable. This murky individual was established in the entrance to an old and abandoned tunnel. A kerosene lamp, set on a rock, provided meagre illumination. Recently washed trousers dripped from a line. On a natural shelf in the rock there was a bachelor nest of blankets. An iron pan sat on an outdoor fire; there was a powerful aroma of frying goat-flesh.

'If it's as good as it smells,' Jim said, 'that's a fair sort of meal.'

The stranger was quick to his feet.

'Who's that?' he said, straining to see across firelight. Then his eyes discovered Jim. With rifle slung on his shoulder, Jim may have looked inhospitable.

'I could ask the same,' Jim said. Sidestepping the fire, he found himself facing a distinctively formed Maori. The fellow had the build of a barrel on stilts, mostly torso, his legs long and skinny. His condition wasn't any more elegant. Not only was he threadbare. His clothes were filthy, his hair long and matted with mud and forest leaves. He was also all twitches, his eyes especially mobile. His bruised face suggested that he had just survived ten punishing rounds with a brick wall. He made no move to anything which might make a weapon, though a shotgun and rifle sat near.

'The name's Dave Smith,' Jim said, extending a fraternal hand.

The gesture left the Maori undecided. 'You wouldn't be looking for me?' he asked.

'Should I? Jim asked.

The Maori shrugged. 'Some are,' he explained.

'You're on the run, then? Is that what you're saying?'

'Something like that,' the Maori acknowledged. 'So you reckon you haven't heard of me yet?'

'It might help if I had a name.'

'They call me Mad Matt,' the fellow said.

'It doesn't mean much to me,' Jim confessed.

The stranger seemed disappointed.

Jim hastened to explain, 'We don't hear much of anything hereabouts.'

'We?'

'Me and my lady.'

The Maori gave a low whistle. 'You mean you live up here? With a woman?'

'Nowhere but,' Jim said.

'You're telling me the truth, then? You're not carrying handcuffs?'

'Me?' Jim laughed.

'You.'

'If I'm getting your drift,' Jim said, 'it's all to the good that I've never heard of you. Have I got that right?'

The Maori thought for a moment. 'I reckon,' he smiled.

'Another thing,' Jim said, 'if you want to keep out of harm's way on the Coromandel, you've just met the right neighbour. For a start, there are more comfortable holes in the hills. This one's likely to leave you wet-arsed in winter.'

'How would you know?' the Maori said with interest.

'Because I tried it for size early on.'

'This place? Early on?'

'When I had need of a hideout myself.'

That impressed the Maori. 'You too,' he said.

'So take my tip. There are other mine entrances more dry, and even more out of the way.'

'Thanks,' the Maori said.

'And your problem's your own,' Jim added, 'unless you need to make it mine.'

There were only minutes of light left in the sky; the way downhill would soon be difficult.

This time there was a strong handshake.

'By the way,' Jim confided, 'my name's not Dave Smith. Never was. For what it's worth, it's Jim Bird.'

'Should I know it?'

'Not necessarily.'

'So why are you telling me?'

'Because I need to remind myself now and then,' Jim explained. 'Besides, I have the feeling I mightn't have seen the last of you.'

'And you might be right,' Matt said. 'By the way,' he added, 'you folk wouldn't have a liking for oysters and eel?

'I'm partial,' Jim confessed. 'Laurel too. For oysters, that is, maybe not eel.'

Next day the Maori came toiling uphill with a sack of oysters fresh from the sea. Laurel, in return, mustered a slab of cake bursting with fruit. Nothing pleased her more than an appreciative visitor, especially one with a sweet tooth. Matt passed on both counts. She didn't let him leave without a pot of her raspberry jam.

'Maybe we might do some hunting together,' Matt said.

'A mate might be handy,' Jim agreed.

Matt wasn't a mystery for long. (If Jim had bought newspapers, he wouldn't have been one at all.) The silences of the peninsula invited confidences; secrets didn't last long between men stalking bird and beast and rewarding themselves with whisky.

Matt was an inland Maori, from the Waikato, a region named for the wide river which ambles through it. After the Anglo-Maori wars of the 19th century, his tribe's territory had been sliced into tidy portions and used to reward Queen Victoria's soldiery for their exertions. Then the new century came calling. So, soon after, did civil servants with excitable documents, warnings in bold print. These revealed that the recently crowned King of England, one George V, desired their company in distant Europe; there was a war to be won on the Western Front. Since 1916 all healthy men of European colour had been liable for military service; now such conscripts were thinning it was the duty of the Maori to don battle dress for Britain. The most devious of these printed appeals reminded Maori of the armed feats of their ancestors, warriors who had never shirked a call to arms. Such forebears, these documents asserted, were not to be shamed. Tribesmen elsewhere, finding this persuasive, reluctant to be called cowards, were soon arranged in ranks, shuffling this way and that to the shout of hoarse sergeant-majors. Few men of the Waikato were to be sighted among the parading conscripts. Rather than listen to orders and take up rifles, they stubbornly remained at home on the day they were due to begin martial chores. They informed the authorities that they had nothing against Germany's Kaiser; that he had never appropriated an inch of their land. The same couldn't be said of drum-beating politicians perpetuating Britain's past misdemeanours. Tribesmen of the Waikato suggested George V return their lost land, with decent apologies; they might then be ready to give him a hearing. Meanwhile their fight wasn't on the Western Front. Their enemy, if they were obliged to have one, was here. This suggestion could be construed as sedition, and was.

Servants of justice made a last plea to a noisy assembly of intransigents. So too did fellow Maori already attired for war and sporting the rank of lieutenant and captain. These loyalists eventually stepped aside to let the law have its way. Constables in dark garb, batons in hand, hurled themselves at the foremost defaulters. The humiliating click of handcuffs was followed by bitter imprecations. Not all were taken. A half dozen fettered defaulters were sufficient to make a shaming spectacle. Maoris trumpeting old injustice, by way of escaping allegiance to the British Empire, might now think twice.

Never having noticed his connection with Buckingham Palace, Matt was among those arrested. Not conspicuously a hero, nor much of a malcontent, he marvelled that he was considered important enough for handcuffs. Until the constabulary arrived his reputation had never been more than that of an averagely mischievous tribal hothead, often in strife with drink. Far from sure what the current bedlam was about, he stumbled upon fellow tribesmen in fraught confrontation with uniformed men. Lurching clear, he collided with an officious constable. Instinct told him to fend the fellow off. Though he put no great power into his punch, the consequence was a senseless constable with a shattered nose.

The trial was short and Matt's sentence long. In evidence he had been named ringleader, since it was helpful to have a sullen villain on show. He confirmed the prosecutor's allegation with an inflammatory Waikato war cry learned at the feet of a warrior grandfather. Though imperfectly recalled, and faultily delivered, it made his point more than a martyr's speech from the dock. It certainly left a compelling silence. The magistrate eventually remembered to remind Matt that it was still in the power of the military to race him to France when his sentence had been served. There he might face a court martial and then, if he still refused his services, five loaded rifles.

Rushed to prison, Matt remained out of step with the world. His utterances were obscene rather than seditious. After an informal beating, he spent his first fortnight of confinement on restricted diet — stale bread and murky water — in the dark of a befouled solitary cell. He emerged gaunt and unshaven, his waistline leaner, his bloodshot eyes blinking in the unkind light of day. Though he had no desire to repeat it, the experience was instructive; it helped him see much that might have passed him by. Likewise enforced sobriety; it was cruelly long since his last drink. Appearances to the contrary, further tribulation wasn't on Matt's schedule. Celebrity wasn't his first choice either. The longer he withered behind bars, the more likely he was to hear a clang of gate heralding a party of foul-mouthed military police determined to fit him with a uniform and dump him aboard a boat bound for Europe. He didn't trust his luck there. It was poor enough on this side of the planet.

To the awe of prison colleagues he began looking charitably on the world. Insults began washing over him; he took prison's daily slights in his stride. His sour grunt was gone, a sweet-natured laugh in its place. He even managed to bring a little sunlight into the thankless existence of his guards. This suggested that a book should not be judged by its cover, nor a Maori by his police record. Some warders, themselves out of sorts with the world, even shared their lumpy wartime tobacco. According to plan, he was judged a model prisoner, rewarded with a place in an outdoor work party. Then prison gossip told him that a party of military police was arriving to look war defaulters over and win recantations from those weary of viewing the world from behind bars and barbed wire. On that summer day, the great outdoors never greener, Matt leapt from a work party, fracturing the jaw of an overweight warder who failed to bound clear as athletically as his fellows.

Nothing enlivens uniformed humans more than a manhunt. It provides a rare chance to perfect their predatory skills, to pit themselves against two-legged quarry. Anyway the chase was on, and Matt on the rampage. He was reported north and south, east and west, in regions he had never glimpsed, and most of which he never would. Within a hundred mile radius there was hardly a burglary not attributable to Matt. There was not a horse stolen, nor a sheep pilfered, for which the absconding Maori wasn't held responsible. Veteran criminals went unmolested. They welcomed an amateur covering their tracks. Some even volunteered their services for their nearest posse; pickings were healthy when unprofessionally burgled houses were searched for clues to the fugitive. (If Matt left a personal signature, it was usually in the form of an empty bottle.) Early success, leaving northern New Zealand in uproar, meant hubris was likely to undo him. Roughly on schedule, it did. His mistake was to saunter into an unfamiliar district in search of a dry barn. It happened to be a district in fright. Two reports of Matt had been received that day: one of these alarms proved to be a juvenile raiding a plum tree; the other the district's best-known drunk crying tragically from a slimy ditch. The locality was unnerved, awoken, and its male inhabitants, reinforced by mustered constables, out in large number. The din had settled, with a cordon of apprehensive men disposed around the school, the store, and village hall. A less relaxed absconder might have seen the place as suspiciously silent. Matt, however, wandered through the cordon, moving from tree to tree in shadowy moonlight. Then a couple of scrappy trees rearranged themselves with no apparent human involvement. Common sense told him that magic was no explanation. It also informed him that he might be in difficulty. Testing this conjecture, he cupped his hands together and shouted *Shit!* to the sky. This confirmed his fear.

A fusillade followed. Richochet bullets whined around. The racket of discharging rifles mingled with vocal alarm. Aggrieved men were roaring, and one or two groaning. Casualties could well have been larger. One pursuer had taken a shot in the shoulder from a fellow marksman; another had blasted away his big toe. Nevertheless the damage done was enough to lend colour to the district's small stock of lore.

Circumstances suggested it time for Matt to move on. He hadn't stopped moving since. After another mishap involving unhinged constables, which accounted for his fresh bruises, he found himself short of refuge in his native region; he looked elsewhere. In time past his mother's people had lived on and about the Coromandel. They carved coastal hilltops into fortresses designed to discourage enemies; they planted pockets of fertile land with sweet potato; they snared birds and netted fish. There was much to be said for the place, and his mother had said most of it. It might be somewhere to sit out the war. Afterwards, who knew?

'So here I am,' Matt said.

'Maybe it's age,' Jim said, 'but I think I'm growing deaf.'

'Deaf?' Matt asked.

'I didn't hear a word,' Jim explained.

They shook hands.

'Just one thing,' Matt added. 'If you see someone creeping around here, someone who shouldn't, you'd be doing me a favour if you gave me a shout.'

'I'll make it a shot,' Jim promised.

'Thanks,' Matt said.

He took up his rifle. 'So are we hunting today,' he asked, 'or just buggering about?'

By then it was 1918, the final year of the war, though past experience suggested the inhabitants of the Coromandel would be the last to learn. Fever was still rife elsewhere; tears for the dead only fuelled civilian passion. In January that year Jim and Laurel found a familiar face at their door. Bandy was back again. Asthma had ended his duty to the empire; a charitable doctor had rewarded him with final retirement. 'I suspect it was homesickness,' he announced. 'I needed the Coromandel. Friends are the best medicine.'

'I suppose you'll soon be off chasing huia again,' Jim said.

'Not to my way of thinking,' Bandy confessed.

'No?'

'I'm getting too creaky,' Bandy explained. 'The only birds I need now are Laurel and Jim of Grief Gully.'

In 1948 Alice was into her seventies, her daughters middle-aged and most of her grandchildren long-legged adolescents or virtually adult. They camped by stream and sea, caught snapper and picked oysters and collected jasper and agate, carnelian and chalcedony. They also hiked up into the ranges. Alice seldom excused herself from these excursions on the ground of her advanced years. She was also working with watercolours again. There were fresh subjects and old. She even found it possible to take a more charitable view of flowering plants; their sex lives no longer left her yawning.

A week into their holiday they took a steep and mostly overgrown track into the interior. Alice, after barely holding her own for a time, found she could climb no further. Making herself comfortable at the foot of a sufficiently picturesque waterfall, she announced that she planned to sketch until the others returned.

Her grandchildren were unwilling to leave her behind. 'Come on, Grandma,' the youngest pleaded. 'We'll push you uphill.'

Daughter Lucy came to her rescue. 'Sometimes,' she told the children, 'Grandma needs to be alone with her memories.'

It was true that Alice liked to be alone with pen and brush. Memories didn't have to be sought. They arrived unbidden as she worked. Sooner or later she fancied all her dead at her shoulder. (She had now outlived three husbands and a fourth would soon join that fraternity.)

The summer day drifted past. Alice was in serene sleep when her grandchildren burst from fern to report an apparition in the hills.

'A what?' Alice said.

'A ghost,' the younger children claimed. 'A real live ghost.'

'Don't talk rubbish,' Alice said severely. 'Ghosts aren't real. Nor, so help me, are they alive.'

'There was one, Grandma, true.'

'What kind of ghost, then?' Alice asked.

'A witchy old woman in fancy dress,' the children explained. 'True, Grandma, true.'

Jane arrived back with the remaining children. All seemed unnerved.

'What's this all about, then?' Alice asked.

'We stumbled on to private property.' Jane explained.

'Private property? Up here?'

'It came as a surprise to us too,' Jane said.

'What's this about an old woman in queer dress?'

'We found ourselves looking down into a clearing,' Jane explained. 'There was a little farm among the trees. This woman appeared. Spooky? I expect she was. Her appearance was rather bizarre.'

'Bizarre?'

'Like someone wandered off the set of a period movie. Anyway not of this day and age.'

'Up there?'

'Two or three miles up,' Jane confirmed. 'And while I was struggling to keep the children quiet, a man appeared. A rather elderly, grizzled and grey-haired gentleman.'

'Ghostly too?' Alice was still disposed to mock.

'He wasn't out of the ordinary,' Jane said. 'Yes, and he was carrying a gramophone. One of those old wind-ups with a weirdly large speaker. He wound it up and put on a record. Of all things it was opera. The record was rather threadbare, but produced something recognisable. Musetta's flower song from La Boheme if I heard right. I gained the impression it was something they did often.'

'Puccini in the New Zealand woods?' Alice said. 'Amaze me still more.'

'Very well,' Jane said. 'You wouldn't believe the birds.'

'Birds?'

'By the score. Winging in, circling and winging off again, as if the place was on their daily route. Some were looping the loop; others hovering overhead. Neither human seemed to think it strange. They sat in the afternoon sun, listening to their music and drinking tea. He smoked his pipe; she appeared to be knitting a sweater. There was no mistaking affection between them. Once, in the first-act finale from Traviata, he reached out and placed his hand on her knee. He was slow to remove it. She laughed — a little fluttering laugh — and so did he.'

'While you spied?'

'Not for long. We didn't wish to ruin their little tableau. We made a tactful retreat.'

'I should think so,' Alice said.

'We thought you might have some idea of what a couple of geriatrics might be up to in these hills,' Jane said.

'Why me?'

'As you never fail to remind us, you lived in this vicinity once.'

'Fifty years ago. And only until your father ran off with me. Or me with him. I've forgotten which.'

'So it's a mystery,' Jane decided.

'There was no mystery about it,' Alice said. 'We loved each other.'

'I'm talking about the pair we glimpsed in the forest,' Jane said.

'There may be no mystery there either,' Alice asserted. 'If men and women had no use for each other, Adam and Eve would have frolicked in vain.'

'If you say so,' Jane said.

'I do,' Alice said.

Next morning Alice announced her intention to hike uphill herself. She didn't care for riddles; she was already losing sleep.

'It's hard going,' Jane warned.

'Perhaps the children will help me along,' Alice said. 'We might make a picnic of it.'

There was no shortage of noisy volunteers for a ghost-hunting sortie. In the end Alice was obliged to take them all, leaving their mothers at their campsite to prepare the evening meal. Alice extracted a vow of silence. There were to be no high jinks; there was to be no laughter. She didn't want the sylvan twosome taking fright.

It was near noon when they heard an axe. They soon looked down on a cottage hedged around with fern and second-growth forest. There was smoke from a chimney and washing on a line. In the middle distance there was an aged gentleman splitting sawn logs. There was no one else on show. Alice silently signalled her grandchildren to follow as she eased her way around a bluff, and descended to the clearing. Then she held up a hand for a halt, and went on alone.

The chopping stopped. The man gazed at Alice.

'So who'd you be?' he said, with some suspicion.

'And who would you?' Alice asked.

Her question went unanswered. There was a silence while he tried to sum Alice up. Finally he appeared to decide that he liked the look of her.

'You'd best ask Laurel,' he suggested.

'Laurel?' Alice queried.

'My wife,' he explained. 'She's the expert on who's who around here.' He called toward the cottage. 'Laurel? Laurel? You there? We have a lady caller.'

'I have children with me,' Alice thought to say. 'Do you mind?'

'Mind? Mind children?'

'Some do.'

The man was faintly amazed. 'Not around here,' he informed Alice.

Alice beckoned Jane's brood from hiding. The smaller approached shyly, one by one, their eyes on Jim Bird.

'We're planning a picnic,' Alice said. 'Do you mind if it's here?'

'Make yourself at home,' the man said. He called toward the hut, 'Laurel? Where are you?' To Alice he added, 'She's probably prettying herself. Laurel likes to look well for visitors.'

'What woman doesn't? Alice said.

Laurel stepped from the cottage. Alice later said there was only one word to describe the woman. Queenly, she said. Laurel wore a wide sunhat, a long floral dress, and a vintage fox fur. There was no mistaking her as other than the mistress of this woodland lair.

'My wife,' Jim said with pride.

Laurel advanced on Alice, extending a gloved hand. 'You're expected,' she said graciously.

'Me?' Alice said. 'Us?'

'I always know. The hairs at the back of my neck rise when visitors are near.'

'What else do they say?' Alice asked.

'That's my secret,' Laurel said coquettishly.

It was an enlightening visit. Laurel learned that youngish women now wore shorts, and that even women of middle years were to be seen in trousers. Though she tried to conceal shock, she was even more unsettled by Alice's grandchildren disporting themselves in the briefest of bathing suits before splashing into a cool creek.

Alice had more reason to wonder at the pair before the day ended. At first she wasn't up to believing it. Then she had to. Jim and Laurel had not only seen off one century; they were on their way to surviving a second.

'But no children?' I said to Alice.

'Timms may have made that impossible. I never found the moment to inquire, and anyway Laurel was the last person to ask. One couldn't help noticing that she was happiest baking biscuits for my grandchildren. Isolation never mattered as much to Jim. He had Laurel. And he had mates of sorts — the likes of Bandy and Matt. She had no woman friend, no one she could call her own.'

'Until you,' I suggested.

'A little late in the day,' Alice said. 'At least I was less obstreperous than the company Jim kept.'

'You're talking of Matt?'

'Who else?' she said.

Jim came to regret that he didn't read newspapers. He would have learned that, despite Mad Matt's currently blameless existence on the Coromandel, his atrocities were still mounting elsewhere; at times he seemed accountable for failed British offensives on the Western Front. Jim might also have become aware of the widely told tale that Germany's Kaiser had sent his personal congratulations to the fugitive. 'If you hold the North Island, I'll take the South,' he was said to have promised.

Above all Jim might have learned that a Major George Timms (retired) had, after vigorously petitioning politicians for an active role in the new conflict, been belatedly rewarded not with a regiment in France, which had been his hope, but with a troop of uninspired nondescripts to bully into shape. A mix of aged constables, muscular military police, and twitchy veterans of the Somme, this party was to deal with disobedience where it showed itself in the form of deserters and defaulters, pacifists and agitators. Given past performance as a disciplinarian, Major Timms was judged ideal for this enterprise; there was certainly no one better suited to taming the unruly individual known the length of the country as Mad Matt. His example had become potent. There were more reports of Maori conscripts going to ground, sometimes with dissidents of European colour bedding down beside them.

'We shall put an end to his nuisance in short order,' Timms promised a journalist. 'Any who think to offer him aid and comfort had best beware. They could well suffer the same fate as he.'

Did the Major, the journalist asked, have some idea where the absconder might be?

'An interesting report has just come our way,' Timms said. 'It suggests that an especially wild and woolly Maori has been glimpsed afoot in the Coromandel region — and at least once with a white companion. The description appears to fit our missing man. We mean to comb the Coromandel twice over, if need be.'

'Timms?' I asked Alice.

'You heard me,' she said.

'Shouldn't he be dead?'

'From all possible points of view,' Alice agreed. 'Unfortunately malevolence has its own rhyme and reason. It seems he remained in reasonable working order. Nothing but mercy missing.'

'And you're asking me to believe that he turned up on the Coromandel?' I protested.

'I'm not asking you to believe anything,' she said. 'I'm telling you. Is something wrong?'

'It's a rather astonishing coincidence,' I argued.

'When,' Alice asked, 'are coincidences not?'

'True,' I said grudgingly.

'I can see that it makes you uncomfortable.'

'Perhaps.'

'No doubt you have sceptical readers to consider. And a profound desire not to be seen gullible.'

'It's not that,' I claimed.

'No? If you prefer not to dabble in that realm, you can argue that it's a small world.'

'All the same,' I said stubbornly.

'Call it what you like,' she said with impatience. 'What we mindlessly call coincidence — when events congregate, or names cluster — may just be life tapping us on the shoulder to tell us that there's a rogue symmetry abroad in the world; that life is never more comprehensible than when it isn't. Are you with me?'

'I'm trying,' I said.

Staying abreast of Alice still involved a mental four-minute mile.

On a late summer day Matt and Jim crossed to the far side of the peninsula. Game was not their first interest. Preoccupied with safety and continued serenity, Matt felt a need to make himself more familiar with his surroundings. Jim went along for the ride. Putting forest behind them, the pair descended to a peaceful bay, all white sand and silver sea, with distant crayfish pots bobbing and waves slapping on the hull of a red sailing dinghy. At an extremity of the beach there were a few weathered cottages, the remnant of a goldfield township. Aside from the tethered dinghy and the crayfish pots, there was nothing to say the place saw much of the human race; the horizon was as lifeless as the shore.

'Seen what you want to?' Jim asked.

'I reckon,' Matt said.

'Not that there's much to see anyway,' Jim observed.

'I wouldn't say that,' Matt said.

'What would you say, then?'

'It's handy to know where the back door is.'

'For a change of scene?'

'A quick one,' Matt said.

'The worst mightn't come to the worst,' Jim argued.

'Maybe,' Matt said without conviction.

There was a dimly familiar foreboding in his tone. Then Jim identified it. He had once heard it in Luke Perham's voice when he felt life's clock ceasing to tick. 'We're too exposed here,' he told Matt. 'Let's head home.'

Matt, however, wasn't in a hurry to call off his reconnaissance. He looked out to sea, shading his eyes against glare. Verdant islands and rocky islets shimmered off-shore. Jim's gaze remained landward. For a moment he imagined he saw the flash of glass — perhaps of binoculars or telescope — from the far end of the shore. Then, since nothing further stirred there, he decided it must be sun on a window. If not, Matt might soon be on the move again.

'What's out past those islands?' Matt asked.

'Mostly water,' Jim said.

'What about Africa?'

Jim was perplexed. 'Africa?'

'Where you were. It must be out there too.'

'You could say that,' Jim agreed. 'Pretty much every place is.'

'If I headed out there, how long would it take to hit land?'

'Something on the far side of a hundred years.'

That impressed Matt. 'So it's a long way,' he decided.

'A fair swim,' Jim said.

'Too far for anyone to come looking?'

'Especially with the world in the way.'

There was a long silence.

'So what are you thinking?' Jim asked.

'When they finish the Kaiser, they could start in on me.'

'You haven't done badly.'

'I'd do better with wings,' Matt said.

Bandy had always been the possible flaw in Matt's arrangements with Laurel and Jim. Perhaps Bandy and Matt were bound to collide sooner or later. It happened on a sunny late autumn day with a faint chill of winter. Matt had grown careless again, taking fewer precautions. If he suspected that Jim and Laurel were entertaining a caller, he sidled off into the trees until the caller, if any, was gone. That day, as if arguing with fate, he departed from custom. He sauntered into Grief Gully without determining the way clear.

Bandy sat on the verandah with Jim, a bottle of home brew between them. Matt could still have backed off before he was seen. The home brew, after a dry hike, proved more interesting than precaution.

'Jim?' he called.

'Matt,' Jim said with surprise.

Matt closed with the two drinkers.

'And this is Bandy,' Jim added. 'Bandy, Matt.'

Jim fetched a third glass and filled it as his guests shook hands. Bandy, however, soon began behaving queerly. He didn't — or couldn't — meet Matt's eye. And he was suddenly shaky, with beer slopping from his glass.

'You're all right?' Jim said.

Bandy was barely able to answer; he looked about to faint. 'Asthma,' he said in a whisper. Laurel came running. She, Jim and Matt managed Bandy indoors and eased him on to a couch. It was some minutes before his hoarse breathing ceased; his trembling took only a little longer to leave. Jim, in his years on the Coromandel, had never seen asthma attack Bandy with less preliminary, or with more venom. Nor did it customarily finish with him so soon.

'I'd best be getting on,' Bandy said with urgency.

'Get yourself together first,' Jim urged.

Bandy was not persuaded to loiter. He fetched his horse; Jim helped him into the saddle. Matt was out of earshot, talking to Laurel. Bandy could risk speaking to Jim.

'You know who that is?' he asked, meaning Matt.

'Do you?' Jim inquired.

'Who doesn't? There's not a week when his photograph isn't in the papers. There's a reward out.'

'For much?'

'It started off at fifty pounds,' Bandy said. 'They could be bidding five hundred now.'

With Bandy gone, Jim relayed this conversation to Matt. Matt, however, showed no inclination to test the waters elsewhere; he didn't retrieve his horse and ride home, as he might have, to his native Waikato. 'I'll sleep on it,' was all he promised.

More surprise was on the way. Back in town, Bandy found uniformed men, rifles slung on their shoulders, stationed at both ends of the main street and, for good measure, in the middle too. They were halting townsfolk and travellers and asking questions. The significance of this activity wasn't lost on Bandy. From here on, matters were bound to take a miserable turn.

A constabulary sergeant waved Bandy down. To the rear of the constable was a man of menacing authority, a heavily built officer with bristling moustache; he required Bandy's attention. 'You may well be able to assist with our inquiries,' he explained.

'Me?' Bandy said, his mouth dry.

'You,' the officer said.

He passed Bandy a circular which announced that a military defaulter and prison escaper commonly known as Mad Matt was wanted by the law for, among other things, grievous bodily harm and attempted murder. There was an unflattering photograph of the runaway.

'You ever seen this man? said the officer.

Bandy began shaking again. His breathing also grew conspicuous.

'Never,' he asserted, a little too intensely.

'Look again. You quite sure?'

'Extremely sure,' Bandy replied between wheezes.

'With respect,' the officer said, 'you are now holding the photograph upside down.'

Bandy was. His temperamental hands continued to have a problem with the picture; he couldn't stop it flapping.

'If you see anyone resembling this brute,' the officer went on, 'I should be grateful if you could report instantly to me. The name is Timms, by the way. Major Timms.'

'I'll remember it,' Bandy stuttered.

He led his horse away, trying not to look over his shoulder.

Timms turned to a police sergeant at his side. 'A funny sort of fish,' he observed.

'Yes, sir,' the sergeant said.

'And more than a mite jumpy, wouldn't you say?' Timms went on.

'He acted strange,' the sergeant agreed.

'Intuition tells me, sergeant, that he might be worth our attention. We've seen no one else likely. If this confounded Maori is around, it stands to reason that some local must know.'

'Possibly, sir.'

'And it might just be this customer,' Biggs suggested, nodding toward Bandy's back. 'Have your men keep an eye on him. See what they learn.'

It was noon next day before Bandy judged himself ready to risk a clandestine excursion to Grief Gully. Jim had to be warned. Mad Matt too. Though Bandy had mixed feelings about the Maori, he deserved consideration as a mate of Jim's. Mateship and its virtues often figured large in Jim Bird's rhymed lines; the message had never been lost on Bandy.

Uniformed men were still posted the length of the main street; Bandy took a back route. To his rear, two men, one with binoculars, mounted their horses and began following discreetly and rather too slowly. It was plain that they weren't much taken with the prospect of meeting up with Mad Matt. Meanwhile vegetation hid their man. Hoofprints grew less useful as the track divided, divided again, and delivered them into unfriendly bushes of nettle. Jim's labyrinth had never served its purpose better. It was late afternoon before Bandy's pursuers cursed back to town. Unsuspecting Bandy, reaching Laurel and Jim hours earlier, had no cause for another asthma attack. He also managed to convey his news without a stutter; he said all he had to say about Mad Matt. There was more to tell, of course. More was the man who questioned Bandy. More was an officer named Timms.

'Timms?' Jim said.

'That's what he called himself,' Bandy said.

'You're sure?'

'As sure as God made green apples,' Bandy said.

He didn't make sense of the ensuing silence. Laurel seemed about to speak and failed to. Jim was equally wordless. It was as if Bandy had uttered an obscenity. 'Is something wrong?' he asked.

'Not yet,' Jim insisted. 'We're glad of the warning.'

'You know this fellow Timms?' Bandy said.

Jim looked to Laurel. Laurel looked to Jim.

'We're acquainted,' Jim admitted.

'Acquainted? In what way?'

'In the worst way,' Jim explained. 'Otherwise what you don't know won't hurt you.'

'Can I help?' Bandy asked.

'By getting home before dark,' Jim suggested.

'What about you? You and Laurel?'

We're overdue a holiday from Grief Gully anyway. We might find a quiet cove to pitch a tent.'

'And Matt?'

'You've never seen him.'

Bandy made his way back to town. His return didn't go unobserved.

'Would you like me to bring him in for questioning, sir?' the police sergeant asked Timms.

'I think we can forgo that, sergeant. We now know where he enters and leaves the forest.'

'Sir?'

'If the Maori persists hereabouts, he's probably warned and about to bolt,' Timms said. 'Have men mustered at first light.'

'What then, sir?'

'We have thirty rifles,' Timms said. 'It is also reasonable to presume that we are better supplied with ammunition. We'll use that advantage to make him break cover. If we don't flush him out tomorrow, then no one will.'

'You're talking about shooting on sight, sir?'

'I imagine I am, sergeant,' Timms said.

By morning, with belongings stowed and packhorse burdened, Jim and Laurel were ready to abandon Grief Gully. Jim meant to take a meandering path across the peninsula, alerting Matt along the way. Aside from leading Timms a dance across difficult terrain, and remaining out of range of his men, Jim had no plan. Knowledge of the peninsula was their advantage. He and Laurel, Matt too, were about to become Boers.

This was soon confirmed. They had barely cleared Grief Gully when they heard the first shots. These were from their rear, off to the east. The next, also to their rear, were from the west. The third discharge, from the north, was placed in the space between earlier volleys. As deafened birds took wing Timms' design became clear. He was cautiously filling the forest with shot before pushing men uphill. This bull-at-a-gate tactic may have been lacking in invention; it wasn't in ferocity. Birds circled even more thickly overhead.

Jim found decision made. Turning back was out of the question; he and Laurel might put themselves in the path of a volley. They had to keep ahead of Timms' rifles. 'Hurry,' he told Laurel, slapping their horses ahead. By then voices could be heard, Timms' most audibly; he and his men were trying to stay in touch with each other as they fought through creeper and fern to place staggered volleys. Jim and Laurel may have begun a half hour ahead; it was soon less, and Laurel was flagging. Jim glimpsed a familiar height ahead. Its scrubby summit might have something to be said for it as a sanctuary. At the least it might give them a view of events. They tethered their horses in a grove of surviving kauri, splashed through a stream, and began climbing. Eventually they had a large view of the peninsula, with sea left and right and tall trees at their feet.

Shot continued to echo from hill to hill. The wanton use of ammunition suggested that Timms was still in search of a battle he could win. Smoke, wisping up through greenery, marked his route through the forest.

Then there was a solo shot. From the south, roughly.

'Matt?' Laurel whispered.

'He can't take on an army,' Jim said with some pain.

There was a short silence in the shot's wake. A second and third, from the same locality, verified that Matt wasn't being playful. Timms and his men went to earth as twigs splintered and leaves showered around. Timms called up rifles in reply.

'Is there nothing we can do?' Laurel asked.

'Only something stupid,' Jim said.

He got to his feet, nevertheless.

'What are you doing?' she said.

'Something stupid,' he explained.

'What am I supposed to do?'

'Nest out of sight until I'm back,' he said.

He passed her his rifle.

'You're not taking it?' she asked.

'A bullet mightn't stop him. A fright might.'

'What does that mean?'

'You keeping out of the way,' he said.

'Jim,' she appealed.

But Jim had rustled away beyond fern and leaf.

The gusting smoke suggested Timms' party was pushing Matt into a corner, shutting him off from the coast. If so, Matt would soon have trouble on two fronts. Jim scrambled along a ridge until he had a view of the affray as it flickered around rock and tree. Timms and most of his men were moving forward, from one scrap of cover to another, trying to outflank the fugitive. Then, on Timms' signal, they dropped silently from view. Their intention was apparent to Jim from his overhead perch; it couldn't be to Matt at ground level. The silence was meant to make Matt curious. It did. He had to chance learning what Timms was about; otherwise he might find himself encircled. After ten minutes, all of them tense, he shuffled warily into view, making himself a target for thirty rifles.

What happened then was never clear. Even participants made no sense of it. Shadowy behind leaves, Jim was never seen or suspected; his shout was spectral, floating down from nowhere. 'Files about, retire!' he called with authority, '*Files about, retire!*' Not having heard the order, nor given it, in a dozen years, Timms was transfixed. He may have been back on the veldt, ducking Boer snipers. He may even have been at the graveside of a forgotten trooper named

Perham. It added up to incaution. Without thinking, he lifted his head to see further. In the same moment he met shot. Some said one. Others, perhaps tallying the echo, thought two. One was enough. Timms slumped from concealment and lay still.

'Whose shot?' I asked Alice.

'My understanding was that it was never determined,' she said.

'Never?'

'Consider the suspects. Jim Bird, as we know, was carrying no weapon; he can be ruled out. So can Bandy Higgs; he didn't know one end of a rifle from another. It may have been a misplaced shot from one of Timms' more excitable men, which wouldn't have been surprising. Naturally, however, it was put down to Matt. No matter that some evidence at the inquest suggested that the shot didn't appear to come from his direction. Matt was now wanted for murder.'

'And what happened to him?'

'That was never agreed either.'

'Never?'

'Since he wasn't inclined to make himself available to judge and jury.'

There was a silence. 'Talking of Timms,' I said, 'you seem to have forgotten one suspect.'

'You noticed?' Alice said.

'I couldn't not.'

'All is forgiven,' she said. 'You may kiss me goodnight.'

With their commander's body slung across a horse, Timms' men were unanimously of the view that there was no future in warring with Mad Matt; they pointed themselves toward the town. Their obscenities and recriminations waned as they crashed downhill. Their departure allowed Jim to look for Laurel. She was not as he left her; she had wilfully ignored his instruction not to move. She was now resting behind a log. Her situation must have given her a clear view of proceedings, and particularly of Timms. Her eyes were still unnaturally bright. A cooled rifle lay across the log. A feeble ray of sun lit the spent shell at her feet.

'I did what you said,' she announced.

'Did what?' he asked.

'Thought it into the target,' she said.

'I reckon you did,' Jim judged.

Laurel never found need for a firearm again. As she put it, she had only the one shot to fire. It was that or nothing. It wasn't nothing.

Two days later, when Timms' leaderless band had been recalled from the Coromandel, Jim Bird looked for Matt. He knew the route Matt must have taken, and to where. Footprints, travelling toward the coast in single-minded fashion, confirmed that a lone traveller had lately passed that way.

The vista, at the end, was much as he remembered. White sand, lapping water, crayfish pots bobbing off shore. There was one change. The red sailing dinghy which rocked there was gone. It left an eloquent gap.

'Good luck,' Jim whispered, as though there was someone to hear.

Later, footsore and slow, he hiked home to Laurel.

'Is there more to it?' I asked Alice.

'As you seem never to have noticed, the best tales know where to stop.'

'You suggest he wasn't seen again.'

'Not in that decade or the next.'

'You mean he *was* seen? Eventually?'

'If you give credence to rumour.'

'Which you do?'

'Let us imagine that a rather portly gentleman from a far country, well-dressed and dark-skinned, turned up on the peninsula many years later. Let us suppose that the same greying gentleman looked over Grief Gully and found debris where a dwelling once stood. Let us further suppose that he located two unmarked graves side by side in the town cemetery. This free-spending fellow was soon gone.

Before he disappeared, however, he paid a local tradesman for a gravestone. Jim and Laurel Bird were no longer anonymous. *Matt's Friends*, a cryptic inscription said.

'And the mystery visitor was Matt?'

'The fellow allowed it to be thought that he was mulatto rather than Maori; he also did nothing to quash the rumour that he was a self-made merchant who had profited greatly in central America and done rather well in Venezuelan oil. Who knows? It is too unlikely not to be true. At the time his connection with the peninsula was never explained; it was thought that he might have been among the men of many nationalities who once chased gold there. It was some time before anyone comprehended the significance of the gravestone. The cranky couple of Grief Gully were largely forgotten. If Matt himself was recalled, it was chiefly by way of a ditty, sometimes recited in pubs, titled *The Ballad of Mad Matt*, author unknown. For all its faults, incidentally, it pictured the last stand of Major Timms with some authority. Not long ago an earnest local historian, sifting through Coromandel lore, came upon the graves. This romantic fellow was never in doubt that the enigmatic visitor was Matt himself. His hypothesis was that Matt had borrowed a boat and been blown out to sea. Then he may have been picked up by a passing ship, with a skipper who had no intention of turning back to Auckland just because a waterlogged native had been heaved aboard. Matt might have been made to earn his keep as a deckhand. Shipping records suggest that there was a vessel two days out of Auckland, bound for Panama, in the vicinity at that time. You are not, by the way, expected to believe a word of this.'

'I'll keep that in mind,' I promised.

'You'll need to,' she said.

Alice dozed in her favoured armchair for some minutes. Then her eyes opened. 'Expressions of interest remain welcome,' she said.

'In connection with what?'

'In connection with Jim and Laurel. You have yet to ask the large question.'

'Such as?'

'Whether they married. Doesn't it interest you?'

'I took it they must have,' I said.

'They might easily not have. Jim never rushed things.'

'Meaning what?'

'Ten years. After downing an alarmingly large dose of whisky at breakfast one morning he rode to town, picked up a licence, arranged a date with a clergyman, and hurtled home to advise Laurel of his intentions. There was no explanation for the delay and none especially needed. By that time, and for the rest of his life, Jim was comfortable with the surname Bird again. Perhaps some grey-haired fellow countrymen recalled his ballads, perhaps even one or two on the Coromandel, but not many. There were just enough guests — something short of a dozen — to make the event lively. Bandy was the best man. Were there ghosts at the feast? Few ever learned that Laurel had been Timms' widow; the same few knew to keep their mouths shut. Otherwise her link with that woodland fracas in 1918 was never noticed. Or, if it was, it was one too rich in serendipity to be credible. One might argue, on the other hand, that it was skilfully arranged. That fate, perhaps, had placed a bait in the form of Mad Matt; and that fate's bait had been taken. Otherwise, I fear, there is a God.'

Again Alice dozed briefly. Again her eyes opened. 'As for heaven,' she added, 'though I personally find the prospect less than enthralling, some deserve the best seats in the house.'

'Are you still talking about Laurel and Jim?' I asked.

'I am. They died, of course. People do.'

On a midwinter day near the close of the 1950s Jim Bird made his fortnightly ride to town with a packhorse roped to the rear of his ambling mount. These expeditions, a familiar sight for five decades, took twice the time now. This was not altogether attributable to decrepit horses; Jim was now in sight of his eightieth year.

Some time in the early afternoon he was seen tethering horses and transacting business at the bank. A little later he was in the grocer's, stacking provisions into saddle bags. At three or soon after he bought his usual case of whisky at the pub, along with Laurel's sweet sherry. Chocolates and cigarettes weren't forgotten either. No one remembered seeing him leave town, but it was surmised that it was in the vicinity of four p.m. Not that the precise times mattered greatly. What mattered was that the hour was late, the day short, and the journey back to Grief Gully long.

At Grief Gully, as dark came, Laurel began to wait. Hours later she was still waiting. She built up the fire and kept her husband's meal warm until it shrivelled to inedible scraps. Now and then she went to the door, pushed it open, and called his name. Long before morning Laurel was ready for her largest journey since she and Jim found their roost on the Coromandel. In short, she was going to town. If she couldn't find Jim, she could find help.

The track out was in need of clearing and often indetectable. Without a landmark to lead her, Laurel was as good as lost by the time she had gone a mile from home. Even with Jim, she had seldom strayed further; she was in strange territory. More to the point, there was no sight or sound of Jim as she stumbled downhill, tripping on tree roots and finding her feet painfully again.

Trees were slow to part. She was sighted near noon, splashing across a creek, by a farmer fencing acres on the fringe of the forest. She was staggering, frequently falling, and calling out feebly. It was the most unearthly happening in this farmer's life. He would recount it for years, always with wonder. Laurel had dressed her best for her first trip to town. Even dripping mud, she was unmistakably a gentlewoman.

In less than an hour search parties were mustered and moving upland. By the day's end Jim's horses were found. Jim wasn't, not that day or the next. More determined investigation was needed. So were powerful torches and strong ropes. With feet fighting for a grip, men lowered themselves down deep mine-shafts, looking for life. On the third day they sighted an eerie glimmer of flesh in the beam of a torch. Lowering themselves further, the searchers looked down on an elderly and surprisingly tranquil face. Jim Bird's body was wedged in rock. It took two hours to free it from the grip of the peninsula, from creation's detritus and humankind's rubble. Reconstructions of the accident suggested that Jim had become separated from his horses in the early winter dark; that he had stumbled off the track to look for them and found oblivion underfoot. One theory was as good as another; the town constable saw no suspicious circumstances and there weren't. With that settled the body of Jim Bird was borne back to town. His widow was waiting.

'Do you need me to go on?' Alice asked.

'If you can,' I said.

'What does that mean?' she challenged.

'There's nothing that can't wait.'

'Are you suggesting that I'm not up to it?'

'At this hour,' I said.

'Get the gin,' she ordered. 'Let's see who lasts.'

If Laurel made no return to Grief Gully, it wasn't for want of trying. After Jim's death and burial, townsfolk took her in, one family after another. The experience wasn't comfortable for guest or hosts. Laurel viewed her surroundings with suspicion. She was terrified of the telephone, motor vehicles, electric light and taps gushing hot water. The devices of the 20th century, however, were not her only problem. Lack of chocolate and sherry was a more considerable grief; her hosts often lived without extravagance or, worse, were austerely teetotal. Her cigarettes were also frowned on, especially her perilous smoking in bed; she could be heard talking to herself through sleepless and, for her hosts, nervous nights. Laurel's many attempts to flee back to Grief Gully bred more complication. Sometimes a search party was needed, much as the one for Jim. Unlike her late husband, she was found intact, merely exhausted, her head between her knees. Only one person was sometimes able to talk sense to her, that person being an aged Bandy Higgs. When one family after another found Laurel an impossible guest, Bandy took her into his cottage until he also found her too great a burden. Finally he joined forces with the town doctor and had Laurel admitted to the geriatric ward of an Auckland hospital. There was no other institution available to cope with her wild-eyed condition. There too she attempted escape, but the city streets into which she fled proved more frightening than hospital walls. She gave up quarrelling with her captors; she let herself be seen as senile and infirm.

She was seen in large distress only the once, after the death and burial of Bandy Higgs. She caused some commotion at the graveside by refusing to leave in seemly fashion with fellow mourners. She seemed to be conducting her own ceremony. In the end she was steered firmly away so the gravedigger could complete his work. Alice became Laurel's one welcome visitor. She sometimes took Laurel home for a day. Such occasions gave Laurel the chance to dress her best. Alice never failed to provide chocolate, sherry and cigarettes. When Alice prepared lunch, Laurel liked to walk the house, looking at paintings, fingering knickknacks and investigating tonics and bottles of scent in Alice's bathroom. Alice presumed that her guest was ridding herself of sour institutional odours. This wasn't a cause for suspicion. Alice was merely grateful to have Laurel composed and sweet-scented at her table. Her guest's serenity, however, stemmed from a source other than an immoderate intake of wine with lunch; it was based on the belief that she still had enough life to outwit the world. In other words, she had reunion with Jim Bird in mind.

Her strategy became apparent on the morning she was discovered unconscious in her hospital room. A stomach pump was raced to her bed and soon set aside. The sleeping pills she had swallowed had done their work. They had been collected, two or three at a time, never in a number inviting concern, from prescriptions in Alice's bathroom; and hoarded until she had enough to fuel her journey back to Grief Gully. This escape was complete.

Alice's time came too. Long deferred afflictions began signalling her end. A letter from her daughter Lucy, in 1972, warned me that Alice was unlikely to live another month. If I wanted to see her mother again, Lucy added, it would have to be soon. The family would understand if I was unable to make the journey. Alice, she said, would also understand.

That was well-meant rubbish. Alice was unlikely to be in understanding mood if I failed to arrive. I mightn't excuse myself either.

Lucy's letter couldn't have found me further from home or more remote in time. Camped with archaeologists among classical ruins on the Asian shore of the Dardanelles, I was researching and writing a lucrative magazine story on Homer's Troy, trying to reconcile literature's most celebrated city with the record. Not that it much matters, but I had at least learned that Troy's lofty towers had no existence outside Homer's song; the place was possibly never more than a commonplace seaside village vulnerable to predatory sea-rovers. If that were the case, Achilles, if he ever rampaged through the real world, was possibly no more than a vicious bully-boy, a braggart pirate, a Timms of his time.

Looking out on Homer's wine-dark Aegean that evening, a drink of similar shade in hand, I found it difficult to understand what I was doing there. Why muse on Achilles when I had the likes of Luke Perham on hand? Why Hector when I had Mad Matt? Why Paris when I had Jim Bird? Why Helen when I had loyal Laurel?

And that wasn't to speak of Alice.

Forty hours later my Air New Zealand jet was circling Auckland city in the Pacific dark, reefs of light unrolling below. Lucy was waiting at the air terminal. Her expression was grave. Half an hour later, with some fast driving, I was with Alice. She was in hospital and making life difficult for doctors, nurses and relatives. On Lucy's plea I was given time alone with my great-aunt; uproar seemed to diminish.

'I imagine it's no use asking you to get me out of here,' she whispered furtively.

'Probably not,' I said

'All you have to do is race me off when no one's looking.'

'To where?'

'There's always the Coromandel,' she said.

'Don't tempt me,' I said.

'Come on,' she persisted. 'Just the two of us. Now.'

'We'll talk about it tomorrow,' I promised.

'If it worries you,' she said, 'elopement isn't half as hard as it looks.'

'It's not that,' I argued.

'No? What is it, then? You think we're a little on the late side?'

'For marriage anyway,' I said.

'Who's talking marriage?'

'It's where elopement usually leads.'

That left her silent.

'Besides,' I added, 'we're always at odds as it is. Think of what marriage might do. We could finish in a divorce court.'

'Let me look after that,' she said. 'I'm not a lawyer for nothing. My first duty would be to counsel reconciliation.'

'You're trapping me,' I pointed out.

'Some hope,' she said.

She grew quiet. I lifted her head and rearranged pillows. Lucy and Jane came and went, most of Alice's grandchildren, and several great-grandchildren.

She roused herself twice before she finally absented herself from proceedings. The first time she said, 'You've been doing rather well for yourself. I've been reading the reviews.'

'Reviews?' I said. 'What reviews?'

'Those lauding your new book,' she said. 'I trust you have no objection to my joining the chorus.'

'Feel free,' I said, though still baffled. There was no recent book in my life; nor had agreeable reviews lately been raining on my head.

'Not that I would call this one perfect,' she added.

'I wouldn't expect it,' I said.

'Nevertheless I don't think I missed much between the first page and the last. Nothing went into the wastebasket.'

'Nothing?'

'Not even when your more verbose paragraphs presented a serious temptation.'

'Praise indeed,' I said.

'None undeserved. I shall have a bone to pick with anyone who dares suggest this book less than your best.'

She dreamed off for a time, with a faint smile. My childhood apprehensions were confirmed. Only a witch could arrange to read a book I had yet to write.

Minutes later she rallied. 'Take my hand,' she ordered.

I found it.

Her voice was small. 'It's been a long life,' she observed. 'It could also have done with trimming.'

'Possibly,' I said.

'On the other hand one might argue that the universe itself is needlessly long-winded. It monotonously makes the same point again and again. Consider the stars. Why so many? A dozen would do.'

'Perhaps,' I said cautiously.

'You aren't just humouring me?' she said with suspicion.

'Too risky,' I said.

'So we'll be off together in the morning?'

'If not before,' I pledged.

It was before. Alice's life ended minutes later, her hand motionless in mine.

There is more.

It is possible that Jim Bird may not have died fast on that midwinter night. It was the medical view that strain on his heart, as he struggled with his numb body, could have killed him — killed him faster, that is, than smashed vertebrae, broken ribs and punctured lungs. Though he must have suffered discomfort — especially with whisky out of reach — there was possibly no pain; there may have been long and lenient delirium. He could have drifted half conscious for a long night and a longer day. There is reason to imagine so, and we shall. Looking up, from the foot of the mine shaft, he glimpsed sky, daylight fading from fern, and stars beginning to gleam. Sound reached him there too. Birds arrived with dawn, some more audible than others, and two most distinctly. He listened with care, hardly daring to breathe. Their impassioned whistling and twittering was not of a sort he had heard before. Bandy should have been here to confirm that extinction might not have the last word. But Bandy wasn't the only one missing out.

'Laurel?' Jim whispered. 'Laurel? Bugger me if it doesn't sound like you on a good day.'

Whose was the opera? Certainly that of a composer served well by his singers. Their duet floated up into the forest, growing faint, until all but their ghosts were gone. By then Jim Bird was too. His last thought was that Laurel couldn't be long behind. Not for the first time, he was willing to wait.

Postscript

The ingredients of this novel were harvested from several sources. I am in debt to Jack Leigh of the *New Zealand Herald* for reminding me of the voyaging lawyer Henry Swan; the staff of the Auckland City Art Gallery and the Auckland Public Library for providing me with material on the painter Ilene Dakin (nee Stichbury); Patrick Holland of Toronto for material on the poet Lawrence Dakin; and that indefatigable folklorist Jim Henderson for calling my attention to the reclusive Chaffeys, not least in his lively chronicle *The Exiles of Asbestos Cottage*. Thanks are also due to Creative New Zealand (formerly the New Zealand Arts Council) for the fellowship which enabled me to finish this novel.

A NOTE ON THE AUTHOR

Maurice Shadbolt is the author of eleven novels, four books of stories and a number of works of non-fiction. Among them are several now considered New Zealand classics. His most recent publications include the highly praised autobiography *One of Ben's* and *The House of Strife*, the third novel in his best-selling and award-winning trilogy of the New Zealand wars.